"Amanda, huh?"

He pressed his mouth to hers, trying to kiss her. Stephanie fought him. She wasn't going to get taken in again. Ted was a loser.

Finally she broke away. She glared into his swarthy face. "Leave me alone, Ted."

He pointed a finger at her. "What if I blow the little scam you've got going here?"

"It's not a scam," Stephanie replied. "I'm finally making good. I'm back in school and I—"

"Amanda?"

She looked around to see Elizabeth standing behind them.

A devious smile crept over Ted's thin mouth. "Amanda, huh?"

New Kid on the Block

NICHOLAS ADAMS

HarperPaperbacks
A Division of HarperCollinsPublishers

HarperPaperbacks   *A Division of* HarperCollins*Publishers*
10 East 53rd Street, New York, N.Y. 10022

Copyright © 1991 by Daniel Weiss Associates, Inc.
and Coleman Stokes
Cover art copyright © 1995 by Daniel Weiss Associates, Inc.

All rights reserved. No part of this book may be used or reproduced in any manner whatsoever without written permission of the publisher, except in the case of brief quotations embodied in critical articles and reviews. For information address Daniel Weiss Associates, Inc.
33 West 17th Street, New York, N.Y. 10011

First printing: February 1991

Printed in the United States of America

HarperPaperbacks and colophon are trademarks of HarperCollins*Publishers*

10 9 8 7 6 5 4

New Kid on the Block

Chapter 1

Amanda MacKenzie gazed out of the bus window at the green countryside. In late August, the wildflowers were thick, and the trees, although still lush with summer foliage, were beginning to show patches of fall color. The seventeen-year-old girl whose pretty face was reflected in the tinted glass of the window had come a long way from Grand Bay, New Brunswick, a town in one of the Maritime Provinces of Canada. She was traveling to a small New England town called Cresswell. She had already put the United States–Canada border behind her, but she was still a good distance from her ultimate destination.

A new life awaited Amanda in Cresswell. She was leaving an unhappy life with her aunt and uncle in Grand Bay. They were severe people who had not really wanted to take Amanda after her parents had been killed in a boating accident. She had never felt welcome in their home. She knew that when they discovered her note on the kitchen table, telling them that she was leaving for a better life, they would be relieved. They would never try to find her.

She sighed, trying to fend off the sense of anticipation she felt. Amanda wanted the long bus ride to be over. She had not been able to afford a plane ticket; it had taken her almost six months to save up for the one-way bus fare. Her travel fund had come from baby-sitting and skipping lunches at school.

But she had done it. Amanda had escaped the nightmare that had been her life prior to her departure from Grand Bay. She would not have to spend another cold winter in the stark house where she was not welcome. She would never have to endure her uncle's stern gaze or feel the sting of her aunt's hand.

Amanda shuddered. It was not so easy to forget them. But she was going to try. She reached into her purse, taking out a pink envelope. She removed a sheet of pink paper from the envelope and began to read the last letter from her pen pal, Elizabeth Henley.

"Dear Amanda, I can't believe it! You're finally coming to Cresswell. I almost died when you accepted my invitation.

"You're coming just in time for the new school year. You're going to be a senior, just like me. I hope we are in some of the same classes. I know English is your favorite subject. Mine, too! I hope we get into Mr. Fern's class. Nobody likes him and everyone thinks he's kind of a bully. But he's really a good teacher and he spends a lot of time on poetry."

Amanda sighed. She had been writing to Elizabeth for more than a year. They had become pen pals through a magazine that was distributed to schools in the United States and Canada. Amanda had written letters to five different people, but Elizabeth was the only one who had answered. Elizabeth's communications had been a lifeline of sorts. They were Amanda's only connection with a better life, the promise of something beyond the coldness of Grand Bay.

"Elizabeth," Amanda said to herself, "how do I deserve to have a friend like you?"

She turned to the second pink page.

"So," the letter went on, "I've cleared things with Mom and Dad. I told them you're part of a program for exchange students. I had to describe you as sort of needy. But they don't seem to care that you don't have money for room and board. The truth is, I think they want another girl around the house. I've told you about my younger sister, who died when she was only five years old. I've come to think of you as a sister. I hope you don't mind."

A tear flowed out of Amanda's eye. She had never had a brother or sister. She had been an only child.

"We have a big house. And there's plenty of space. You'll have your own room and bath. It's going to be great!"

"I can't wait," Amanda whispered, wiping her eye. She almost broke down. It sounded as though she was going to be part of a real family. She would no longer have to feel like an unwelcome visitor in her uncle's home. Holidays would be bright and cheerful. She could feel the warmth pouring off the pink page. She continued to soak up the friendly words.

"When you get here, Amanda, I'll show you around. Cresswell really is a nice place. You'll love it here. Cresswell High is a good school. I'm chairperson of the decorations committee for the homecoming dance. But that's not until October."

"Homecoming," Amanda said.

She had never been to a dance. Her aunt and uncle wouldn't allow her to see any boys. She had told Elizabeth all about it in her letters. She was going to have a real life in America.

"I was elected to student council last year," Elizabeth had written in her exacting hand. "We have elections in homeroom. I hope I get to be on the council this year. I also love to sing. I was in glee club last year. You said you don't like singing, but I could help you. Tryouts aren't until spring, so we'd have a lot of time. I also sing in the church choir. That would be a good place for you to learn. It's going to be so great. But I'll tell you all about Cresswell when you get here. See you then. Love, Elizabeth. P.S. Have a good trip."

Amanda folded up the letter and put it back in her purse. She had a whole sheaf of letters from Elizabeth. She had saved every one and carried them in her purse as if they were scripture. They were her deliverance, the passport to a better, happier life.

As the bus rolled along the interstate highway, Amanda leaned back in the seat. It was a bright morning. She had slept most of the night, waking in a strange place. She wished there were some way she could snap her fingers and appear in Cresswell. But she would just have to tough it out.

She closed her eyes for a moment. The image of her uncle's face loomed in her mind. Suddenly Amanda was seized by a fear that something would go wrong. What if her aunt and uncle came after her?

Amanda took a deep breath. They wouldn't be able to find her. She had said in her note that she was going across the country. She wanted them to imagine somewhere far away and not have a chance of finding her if they tried.

They hadn't even known about her letters from Elizabeth. Amanda had had Elizabeth send all of her letters to her in care of general delivery at the Grand Bay post office. She had picked up the letters once a week and kept them in her book bag, away from her aunt's prying eyes.

Amanda shivered, trying to put her kinfolk out of her mind. She was free. She intended to stay that way.

The bus pulled off the interstate, taking an exit into another small town. It seemed to Amanda that they had stopped at every town along the highway. Now they were in Wannamoisett, just two hours from Cresswell.

The bus rolled up to a tiny convenience store. Amanda sighed when she saw the clock through the store window. It was noon. She had been traveling for more than twelve hours. It might as well have been twelve days. She couldn't shake the feeling that she would never get there.

After the passengers used the facilities and made some purchases, a few more passengers began to climb onto the bus. When Amanda looked up, she saw a young woman walking down the aisle. Her face was pretty. She had long brown hair. She wore a leather jacket and jeans that were ripped at the knees. The girl sat down in the seat across the aisle from Amanda.

"Hello," Amanda said, smiling.

The brown-haired girl didn't reply. But Amanda was sure she would make friends with her soon enough.

Chapter 2

When Stephanie Rendall boarded the bus in Wannamoisett, she was running away from a life she no longer wanted to lead. Stephanie, who had just turned eighteen, had been dating Ted Dorak for nearly six months. It had taken her almost a month to make her break from Ted, but she had finally gotten up the courage to flee.

As soon as Stephanie sat down in her seat, the straight-looking girl across the aisle tried to pull her into a conversation. Stephanie rolled her eyes and ignored the girl. The last thing she needed was someone trying to cozy up to her. Stephanie leaned back in the seat, hoping the girl didn't belong to some sort of cult and persist in trying to strike up a conversation.

Stephanie couldn't fall asleep, even though she had been awake all night. In her troubled mind, she battled images of her life with Ted. He was older than she by two years. When they had first met, Stephanie had thought he was ruggedly handsome. He was tall and muscular, with black hair that was slicked back. He smoked cigarettes and sometimes looked like James Dean when he dangled a cigarette from his lips.

Stephanie had been dating Ted since her junior year, much to her parents' disapproval. Ted lived on his own, yet rarely had a job. His casual, free-spirited way of life had seemed attractive at first. But it hadn't taken her more than a few months to realize that Ted was lazy, mean-spirited, and totally unmotivated. Her parents had been right all along. By the time she wanted to break up with Ted, it was too late. She had been an accomplice in three of his burglaries, even if it only meant driving the car and waiting for him while he took the loot to a fencing operation.

When she had told him she wanted to break off their relationship, he threatened to tell her parents about her illegal activities and make it impossible for her to return home.

"You're with me now, honey," he said. "You can't go back to your nice, clean little life."

She had known he was right. She couldn't bear to talk to her parents about what she had done. She didn't want them to know how bad her life had become. She had to start fresh.

"Would you like half a sandwich?" Amanda asked.

Stephanie sighed, trying to ignore her, as the bus rolled back onto the interstate.

"It's only olive loaf," Amanda went on. "But you're welcome to it if you'd like it."

Stephanie heard her own stomach growling. She had not eaten breakfast. Her nerves had taken most of her appetite before her middle-of-the-night departure. She hadn't been hungry until now.

And here was this wide-eyed kid, offering her something to eat. The practical side of Stephanie's nature began to take over. After all, she had less than twenty dollars to her name. Better to eat the free food rather than spend money later.

"Well," Amanda said, "if you don't want it—"

"No," Stephanie replied. "I mean, okay. I'll take it."

Amanda smiled. "It's fresh. I made it myself yesterday. I packed fruit and sandwiches before I left New Brunswick. I'm from Grand Bay, but I'm going to a place called Cresswell."

Stephanie took the sandwich from her hand. "Yeah? Fascinating."

Amanda frowned. Stephanie could see that she had been hurt by the flippant reply. They were probably close to the same age, but Stephanie was really older inside, more worldly.

"Sorry, kid," Stephanie replied with a deep sigh. "It's just that—I've had kind of a rotten day. More like a rotten life. I didn't mean anything."

"That's okay. I've had a few bad days myself. Would you like a piece of fruit? I have some soda, too."

Stephanie figured the damage was done. Might as well take the fruit and soda. Maybe she could milk the kid along the way, use her to save money.

"My name is Amanda."

Stephanie sighed, thinking that there was no way out now. "I'm Stephanie."

The girl reached across the aisle to shake hands with her. Stephanie grimaced, thinking that Amanda had just fallen off the turnip truck.

"I'm from Grand Bay, New Brunswick," Amanda said.

"Yeah, I know. You told me."

"Where are you from?" Amanda asked pleasantly.

"I've been around."

They were quiet for a moment. Stephanie tried to close her eyes. She wanted to get some sleep. Maybe when she woke up, the chatterbox would be gone. Maybe life would look a little better than it had for the last six months. Maybe not.

"I hated Grand Bay," Amanda went on. "I lived with my aunt and uncle. They were horrible to me."

"Join the club," Stephanie muttered.

"They don't even know I'm gone," Amanda said. "I slipped out while they were asleep."

Stephanie opened her eyes and looked sideways at the younger girl.

"Do you want another plum?" Amanda asked.

Stephanie shrugged. "Sure, why not."

Amanda handed the plum across the aisle. "Fruit is really expensive in Grand Bay, except in the summer. But I wanted to take a lot of food with me so I wouldn't have to spend any money along the way."

Stephanie bit into the plum. "What do you do?"

"I'm a student," Amanda replied. "I'm going to live with a friend of mine in Cresswell. Here, have a look at her picture."

Amanda dug into her purse. She showed Stephanie a picture of an attractive girl with brown eyes and long brown hair. She also dug out the sheaf of letters, showing them proudly to Stephanie.

"We've been pen pals for a long time," Amanda went on. "Almost a year. I can't wait to meet her."

"Oh?" Stephanie said with growing interest. "You've never met?"

"No. I didn't even have a picture to send her."

"So she's never seen you?"

Amanda shook her head. "No. But I'm going

11

to meet her today. I can't wait to get to Cresswell. I'm going to start a new life."

Stephanie took another bite of the plum, studying the girl more closely. "How interesting."

"Well, I won't bore you with the details—"

"Oh, go ahead," Stephanie replied. "Bore me. Tell me more. I want to hear all about it."

Chapter 3

For the next hour, Amanda MacKenzie talked to Stephanie, and the town of Cresswell was foremost on her lips. Amanda saw Cresswell as some sort of utopia, a place where all her problems would disappear.

The girl seemed to be an inexhaustible font of information. Ordinarily, Stephanie would have been bored with such a tedious, run-on conversation. But as the bus rolled down the interstate, she hung on Amanda's every word. She wanted to learn everything she could about the young runaway.

"I'm talking your ear off," Amanda said apologetically.

Stephanie forced a gracious smile. "Oh, no. It's fascinating. I'd like to hear more."

Amanda had no unvoiced thoughts. She told Stephanie all the details of her life. And Stephanie concentrated intensely, trying to catalogue every significant fact.

Amanda had been born in Grand Bay in 1973.

She was the daughter of a factory worker and a kindergarten teacher. Her parents had been killed when she was twelve years old, the victims of a horrible boating accident. Her father's pleasure boat had been smashed by a tugboat whose captain was drunk. Amanda had been the only one to survive the accident.

When Amanda came out of the hospital, she had gone to live with her Uncle Harville and Aunt Regina. Regina was her mother's older sister. Her father had been an only child, like Amanda. Both sets of grandparents were deceased. Her aunt and uncle were her only living relations.

The death of her parents had put the remains of the meager MacKenzie estate in the hands of her uncle. He had completely mismanaged the funds from her father's life insurance. He had also sold her family's home so he could buy his own fishing boat. But Uncle Harville was a horrible businessman. He had lost everything and had to go back to work as a deckhand. Life for Amanda had been severe and barren thereafter.

Her Aunt Regina was a strict disciplinarian. She had never allowed Amanda to go to school dances. Amanda had never even dated a boy, much less gone steady with one. Her only contact with boys had been at church. Even then, Regina had watched over her like a hawk.

So Amanda had hated life in Grand Bay. She

had always felt cut off from the rest of the world, abandoned to the darkness of winter. Her guardians would not even let her watch television, though they had one in the den.

They would not let her participate in any extracurricular activities at school. Once Amanda had tried to join the poetry club, but when her aunt found her collection of original poems, she had tossed them into the fireplace. When Amanda had protested, Regina had cuffed her with the back of her hand.

There was innocence in the way Amanda spoke. Stephanie couldn't remember if she had ever been that innocent since birth.

"I can't wait to get to Cresswell," Amanda went on. "The Henleys are such wonderful people. Did I show you a picture of Elizabeth?"

Stephanie nodded. "Yes, you did. But I'd like to see it again. Would you show it to me?"

Amanda proudly showed her the picture of Elizabeth Henley. Stephanie took the photograph from her, studying the wholesome face that smiled out at her. It was Elizabeth's junior-year picture, the one that had appeared in the yearbook, Amanda told her.

Elizabeth looked happy and intelligent. Amanda was heading for what seemed to be a life in paradise. She was a babe in the woods, making for the shelter of a perfect American family.

Amanda told her about Elizabeth's scheme to get her to the States and Cresswell. They had worked up a ploy involving a bogus exchange program. Elizabeth had sold her parents on the idea. They were going to accept Amanda into their home. It was all so wonderful.

Stephanie had to admit that the plan was ingenious. "Smart. You two cookies came up with that all by yourselves?"

Amanda nodded. "Like I said, my aunt and uncle have no idea where I went. I'm safe now."

"What if you and Elizabeth don't get along?"

"No chance of that. She's going to treat me like her sister. She had a younger sister who died."

"Oh yeah? What was her sister's name?"

"Helen," Amanda replied. "It was sad. She died of meningitis when she was only five years old."

"Meningitis. Tough break."

There was so much for Stephanie to remember. Amanda was full of facts. And she was all bubbly about her new life.

"Elizabeth told me that Cresswell High is one of the best schools in the state. I can't wait to start there. It's going to be wonderful. And I'll be able to go out with boys for the first time."

Stephanie chuckled. "Boys aren't all they're cracked up to be. They can be a lot of trouble. They use you, take everything you have. They get you in trouble and leave you flat. They'll rip out your heart and throw it away."

Stephanie looked at Amanda, who was smiling sympathetically. Amanda was such a good girl that it made Stephanie sick to gaze into her innocent face.

"What?" Stephanie asked.

"You've had a rough life," Amanda said. "I thought I had it bad, but I can tell you've had it worse."

Stephanie shrugged. "Rougher than most, better than some. I'm still alive."

"You haven't told me much about yourself," Amanda offered. "I'm willing to listen if you need someone to talk to."

Stephanie sighed. "I don't want to bring you down. It seems like your luck is changing. I don't want to jinx you."

"You won't," Amanda replied. "I've gotten this far. Nothing is going to stop me from getting to Cresswell."

Don't bet on it.

A silence fell over them for a while. Stephanie looked around, just to see who had been listening. Their voices could carry on the bus. Luckily, they were the only ones in the back seats. The front of the bus was full but no one seemed to be paying attention to the two girls.

"Hey," Amanda said finally, "would you like another plum?"

"Sure," Stephanie replied. "Break it out."

As Amanda reached for the canvas tote bag on the empty seat next to her, her purse fell off her lap. When the purse hit the aisle, the contents spilled all over the floor. Stephanie saw the sheaf of pink envelopes that had come out of Amanda's pocketbook.

She reached for the envelopes, scooping them up. "What's this, Amanda? You starting a library?"

"I saved all my letters from Elizabeth," Amanda replied. "They're my treasures. Here, I'll take them."

Stephanie's heart was pounding as she handed the envelopes back to Amanda. There must have been more than fifty letters, at least one a week for a whole year. The letters were the final weight that tipped the scale.

Stephanie's plan had finally taken shape. The urge was there, gripping her tightly. She knew she was going to do it.

But as the bus rolled south, they passed a sign that declared Cresswell was only fifty miles away. A sweat had broken out on Stephanie's face. She wanted Amanda's lucky break for herself. But how? She now had to accept the one answer that kept trying to break into her thoughts. She had to eliminate Amanda. She had to kill her. It was the only way.

Could she do it? Her months with Ted had

prepared her for anything. But her plan had to be flawless. Otherwise they would catch her.

Stephanie quickly reached into the pocket of her leather jacket, taking out the bus schedule. There was one more stop before Cresswell: the town of Porterville. It was now or never.

She looked over at Amanda. The girl was dozing with a pleasant smile on her face.

It was then that the final piece of the puzzle fell into place. Stephanie wondered if she could pull it off. Amanda's nap was the key.

Stephanie wiped the sweat from her forehead and braced herself for the unfolding of her heinous scheme.

Chapter 4

The bus rolled off the interstate, heading toward the center of Porterville. Stephanie kept her anxious eyes on Amanda, whose chest rose and fell softly as she slept. Amanda had to stay asleep for a few more minutes. Stephanie's plan hinged on her slumber.

The driver's voice reverberated from the speaker in the front of the bus. "Porterville."

Stephanie grimaced at the shrill intrusion. She stared at Amanda, who stirred in the seat. But Amanda didn't wake up. Her eyes stayed shut.

The driver guided the bus into town. Stephanie felt cold. She drew her leather jacket tighter around her body. Timing was everything. She had to be perfect for her scheme to be successful.

She glanced at the bus schedule she had in her pocket. The bus was due to leave Porterville five minutes after it arrived. Her blue eyes lifted to the clock that sat in the town square. They were arriving ten minutes late. The bus would probably be in and out in a hurry. Just what Stephanie needed.

"This is it."

She took a deep breath. She told herself that it was the only way. A new life awaited her.

The bus hissed and ground to a halt. As soon as it bumped into the station, Amanda opened her blue eyes. She looked immediately at Stephanie.

"We're here," Stephanie said quickly. "You made it, Amanda."

Amanda smiled. "Really?"

Stephanie jumped out of her seat. "Come on, I'll help you with your stuff."

"Thanks."

They gathered Amanda's luggage—two suitcases—from the overhead rack. Stephanie also took her own canvas bag and Amanda's tote. She urged Amanda toward the door, following in her steps.

"Are you getting off here?" Amanda asked.

Stephanie nodded. "Yeah. You made this place sound so good that I thought I'd give it a try."

They shuffled off the bus, emerging in front of the station. Amanda began to look for Elizabeth. Stephanie stood next to her, steering her away from the station sign. She desperately wanted the bus to pull out. It had to leave before Amanda realized they were not in Cresswell.

"I don't see Elizabeth," Amanda said. "I know

she got my letter. She's supposed to be here to meet me."

"We're a little early," Stephanie replied. "Maybe she hasn't gotten here yet. She's probably on the way."

Amanda yawned, still a little groggy from the nap. "Yes, she's on the way. I hope she's all right."

Stephanie kept looking toward the bus, thinking, *Come on. Go!*

The driver was stepping up into the bus.

Stephanie held her breath. *Do it! Get that crate out of here!*

Amanda turned to look behind her, glancing into the station building. "I wonder if she's inside. She could—"

Go!

The driver closed the door.

Amanda's eyes grew wide. "Wait a minute!"

Get out of here now!

"Oh no!" Amanda said.

The bus started to pull away from the station.

Amanda was looking at the station sign. "This isn't Cresswell, Stephanie. This is Porterville."

Stephanie gaped at the sign, feigning surprise. "What? I don't believe it! Porterville?"

The bus was halfway down the street.

"He's leaving without me!" Amanda cried. "Wait! Come back!"

She ran a few steps before she tripped and lost

her balance. She went tumbling to the ground. Her luggage flew in all directions.

Stephanie watched the bus turning the corner, heading back to the interstate. She exhaled a sigh of relief. Stage one of her plan had worked, even if it had been a close call. It was time to move on.

She moved toward Amanda. "Are you all right?"

Amanda shook her head. "Oh, everything's ruined now!"

Stephanie helped the distraught girl to her feet. "I'm sorry, Amanda. It's all my fault. I was sleeping, too. When the bus stopped, I thought we were in Cresswell."

Amanda glanced at Stephanie, who seemed genuinely sorry. "Oh, it's not your fault, Stephanie. It was an honest mistake."

"No, I screwed up, Amanda. How can you ever forgive me? I'm so stupid. I thought this was the stop. When I woke up, I thought I heard the driver say—"

Amanda sighed, putting her hand on Stephanie's forearm. "It's okay." Then she looked closely at her new friend. "You feel so cold."

Stephanie drew back a little. She could no longer look Amanda in the eye, not with what had to happen.

"Let me look at the schedule," Stephanie said

quickly. "Oh no. The next bus for Cresswell is not for another hour. I'm stupid. Totally stupid."

"It's all right," said Amanda. "You were just trying to look out for me. You didn't want me to miss my stop."

"Come on," Stephanie said. "Let's see if we can find a taxi to take you to Cresswell."

"No, that's okay," Amanda said.

"Let's try, at least."

They walked toward the street. Stephanie was counting on a taxi being too expensive. She was right. The fare to Cresswell was almost fifty dollars. Neither one of them could afford it, but Stephanie had come off looking like she truly wanted to help. Amanda continued to have confidence in her.

"I'll just have to wait," Amanda said.

Stephanie frowned. "I feel so responsible. I hope they'll let you back on the bus."

Amanda nodded toward the ticket counter. "Oh, don't be a fussbudget. Let's see what they say about it."

The agent at the ticket window told Amanda that she would be allowed to continue on the next bus to Cresswell. She would not have to pay any extra fare. The bus company would honor her ticket for the last leg of the journey.

Stephanie hung back, not wanting the ticket agent to see her with Amanda. She saw Amanda smiling. So far, everything had worked out fine.

"It's okay," Amanda said. "There's no problem. I'm just going to be a little late getting to Cresswell."

Later than you think.

Stephanie smiled nervously. "Well, I suppose that's all right. I'm still sorry, Amanda. I've got to make it up to you *somehow.*"

"Don't worry," Amanda replied. "I can call Elizabeth and tell her I'm going to be on the next bus."

Stephanie tensed. Another obstacle in her way. She had not counted on Amanda wanting to make a call to her friend.

She followed Amanda to the pay phone. Her nerves had begun to tingle. What if the Henleys decided it was no trouble to drive to Porterville to pick up the newest member of their family? It would rob Stephanie of her big chance.

Amanda stopped at the phone. She reached into her purse, taking out a pink envelope. She looked at the number on the paper. When she dialed the number, the operator came on the line, telling her how much money to deposit.

"Have you got any change?" Amanda asked Stephanie.

"Sorry, no," Stephanie said, mustering a friendly laugh. Either of them could have gotten change easily enough, but Stephanie didn't want to make it any easier for Amanda.

Amanda shrugged. "I'll call collect. Elizabeth

won't mind. I can pay her back after I get my money exchanged."

Stephanie nodded. "Sure."

The operator put the call through. But there was no answer at the Henley residence. Stephanie's luck was holding.

She let out a breath. "Too bad, Amanda."

"I'll bet they're waiting for me at the Cresswell station," Amanda replied. "I've got to get word to them. Hey, I've got it. I can ask the ticket agent to call the station in Cresswell. They can page Elizabeth and give her the message that I'm going to be late."

"Sure," Stephanie said. "Why not?"

Stephanie watched as Amanda related the message to the ticket agent. If the Henleys drove to Porterville to pick up Amanda, Stephanie knew that she wouldn't go through with her plan.

Amanda returned after speaking to the ticket agent. "The agent is going to call the station in Cresswell. She's going to have them tell Elizabeth that I'll arrive in two hours."

Stephanie glanced up, noticing the big map of Porterville on the wall. She studied it until she saw the green patch on the edge of town. It was a place called Arden Glen, a large wooded tract. She knew she had to get Amanda out of the station before the Henleys called back, offering to pick up Amanda at the Porterville Station.

Stephanie smiled. "It's my fault that you're

late, Amanda. Let me make it up to you and take you on a picnic lunch. I'll buy the sandwiches."

Amanda shook her head. "You don't have to do that, Stephanie."

"I insist. Look, there's a place called Arden Glen. It looks like it's just about ten minutes away. We can hike out there and eat our lunch."

"I don't want to miss my bus," Amanda replied.

"You won't. Come on, we can put our luggage in a locker."

"I don't know about this, Stephanie."

"Please, Amanda. It would make me feel so much better."

"Okay," Amanda said finally. "But we can't stay too long."

"Great!"

Stephanie's hands were trembling as she got change for a dollar from a machine and put their luggage in a storage locker. She took the key and put it in the pocket of her leather jacket. When their things were secure, they went across the street to buy some sandwiches.

Stephanie used most of her money for the picnic lunch. But she knew it didn't matter that she was almost broke. Soon she would have a purse full of Canadian money.

They came out of the Porterville Deli and Stephanie guided Amanda toward Arden Glen at the edge of town.

Chapter 5

Elizabeth Henley, a tall, slender girl with dark brown eyes, moved gracefully through the Cresswell bus station. She was a little early. Amanda MacKenzie's bus was not due for another ten minutes. But Elizabeth was anxious to meet her pen pal from New Brunswick.

Elizabeth stopped in front of a mirrored wall, checking her appearance in the smoky glass. Her long brunette tresses hung below her shoulders. Elizabeth took a brush from her purse and nervously ran it through her hair. She put the brush away after a moment and began to study her lovely face.

A wholesome, modest beauty, Elizabeth never wore makeup. Her skin glowed with a natural radiance that other girls envied. Stepping back a little, she regarded her blue dress. It had taken her all morning and most of the afternoon to decide what to wear. She wanted to make a good impression on Amanda.

When she grew tired of looking at her own

reflection, Elizabeth sat on one of the wooden benches in the nonsmoking section. Her eyes kept lifting to the big clock on the wall. The arrival time for Amanda's bus came and went. Elizabeth began to worry. What if something had happened to Amanda?

She hurried to the ticket counter, where she was told that the bus was running ten minutes late. Elizabeth immediately went back to her car and put another dime in the parking meter. Her father had bought her the red Ford Escort for her seventeenth birthday. It was not the most stylish car in Cresswell, but she was sure Amanda would be impressed.

Returning to the station, Elizabeth waited on the wooden bench. As she watched the clock, she continued to worry about other things. Foremost on her mind was the ruse she had conceived with Amanda. Elizabeth wasn't a deceptive person, but she had encouraged Amanda to leave her aunt and uncle. Now that Amanda had run away, it was up to Elizabeth to keep up the charade as long as Amanda was in Cresswell.

Elizabeth wondered if Amanda's guardians would come looking for her when they discovered she was gone. Probably not. They had not wanted Amanda to live with them in the first place. And Cresswell was a world away from New Brunswick. They would probably be glad that she had left them.

Still, there were things to consider, including Amanda's school records from Grand Bay. She had urged Amanda to bring her transcripts with her. That way the authorities at Cresswell High wouldn't have to contact her old school for the transfer papers. If worst came to worst, Elizabeth had a friend who worked in the office during first period. She could appeal to her friend in an emergency.

A shudder played through Elizabeth's shoulders. If someone at the high school in Grand Bay realized that Amanda had transferred, they might have occasion to mention it to her aunt and uncle. After all, Grand Bay was a small town. Then everyone, including Elizabeth, would be in deep trouble. They might come and take Amanda back to New Brunswick.

Elizabeth glanced up as the voice blared over the station loudspeaker.

"Now arriving at gate three, from points north—"

She jumped up and ran toward the platform, watching as the bus pulled in. She could not see the faces inside the tinted windows.

"Where are you, Amanda?"

The passengers began to disembark. Elizabeth kept waiting for her pen pal to get off. But there were no seventeen-year-old girls, pen pal or otherwise.

Elizabeth stepped onto the bus, looking at the

passengers who had stayed in their seats. She didn't see anyone who resembled Amanda.

The driver approached from down the platform. "Where are you going?" he asked.

Elizabeth climbed down. "I'm not going anywhere. I'm looking for someone. Was there a girl with shoulder-length brown hair on the bus today?"

The driver thought for a moment. "I'm not sure. . . . Yes, I think so."

"Did she get off somewhere else?"

The driver shrugged. "I'm not sure where she might have gotten off." He stepped up into the bus, then turned around and looked down at Elizabeth. "A couple of girls got off in Porterville. Maybe she was one of them."

At that moment, the loudspeaker crackled through the station. "Elizabeth Henley, please report to the ticket counter. You have a message. Elizabeth Henley, please report to the ticket counter."

Elizabeth ran to the counter, where the ticket agent told her that Amanda would be arriving on the next bus in two hours. She asked why Amanda had been delayed, but the ticket agent didn't seem to know. She thanked the agent and headed back to her car. She wondered what might have happened, but there was nothing she could do except go home and come back later.

Chapter 6

"This is nice," Amanda said sweetly. "Thanks, Stephanie."

They were walking along the side of the road, next to Arden Glen. Amanda was in front of Stephanie. She had stopped to peer into the green woods.

Stephanie had her eyes on the road. She didn't want anyone to see them go into the forest.

Amanda looked at her wristwatch. "It didn't take long to get out here. Ten minutes. We'd better eat and get back, though. I don't want to miss my bus."

"Don't worry," Stephanie said breezily. "You won't miss your bus."

She was wondering how she was going to do it. Stephanie had a penknife in the pocket of her leather jacket. A stabbing would be difficult and messy, but it might be the only way to do the job.

"There's a path," Amanda said eagerly.

Stephanie nodded. "Let's take it," she said, the hint of a command in her voice.

Amanda didn't notice that her new friend was studying her thin neck. She also didn't notice how nervous her new friend had become.

Amanda started down the path. "This is really a pretty place," she announced.

Stephanie came behind her. No one had seen them entering the forest. Who would report Amanda missing, anyway? When Stephanie took her place, no one would have a clue. The difference in hair styles was a small obstacle, but Stephanie could take care of that. They were roughly the same size. She would fit easily into Amanda's clothes.

They penetrated deeper into the forest. The shadows grew longer around them. Stephanie's sweaty hand clung tightly to the handle of the penknife in her jacket pocket. She wished there was an easier way to do what she wanted to do.

"Look!" Amanda cried. "A brook."

The path widened, opening onto the rocky bank of a babbling brook. Amanda stopped to peer into the clear, frothing water. Then Stephanie fixed her blue eyes on one of the large, smooth stones that rested on the shoulder of the creek.

"This is perfect," Amanda said, putting down the bag of sandwiches and soda. "Let's eat here."

"Sure," Stephanie said, moving over to the stone and pushing it with her foot.

"I've got to wash my hands," said Amanda. She knelt down and moved her hands about in the water of the creek. Stephanie stared at the back of her head. She had to do it quickly, to get it over with.

"The water's cold," Amanda said. "Better not drink it, though. Wouldn't want to get sick."

Stephanie slowly bent down, grabbing a flat, pointed stone that was the size of a dinner plate. Amanda continued to kneel by the water. Stephanie moved closer. She lifted the rock.

Amanda turned suddenly and looked back at her, as if she had had a sudden foreboding that something was going to happen.

Stephanie brought the rock down on the side of Amanda's head. Amanda sprawled to the ground, with only the faintest sound emanating from her throat. Then all was quiet.

Stephanie stood over the body, breathing hard and gazing down at her horrendous handiwork. Amanda was dead, but it was by no means over. Stephanie had to bury her. She stood up, scanning the wooded area for a grave site. Scouting around the perimeter of the clearing, she found some soft earth between two high evergreens. The ground at the base of the trees was covered with brown needles and pine cones that had formed a soft, thick carpet.

It was the perfect spot. Even in winter, when the rest of the forest was bare, the evergreens would still hide the grave. She swept back the needle cover and started to dig.

The grave had to hide the body, so it would never be found. She found a stick to use as a tool.

Stephanie perspired as she excavated the dark earth. There was still a lot to do. She had to get back to Porterville before the next bus pulled out.

When the hole was finished, Stephanie hurried to the creek. Amanda still lay face down near the gently lapping water. The next part was going to be tough. All traces of her own existence had to be erased.

She began to take off her clothes. When she was down to her undergarments, she removed the blue dress from the lifeless body. Then she donned the dress and put her own clothes, including her cherished leather jacket, on the corpse. She kept her money, but she left her identification in the pocket of the leather jacket. If anyone found Amanda's body they would think that it was Stephanie Rendall who had died.

Stephanie dragged the body toward the grave. She laid Amanda to rest in the dark dirt. As Amanda flopped lifelessly into the grave, Stephanie stared hard at the body and tried to get herself under control. Her heart was pounding, and she was breathing hard as if she had just run a mile.

"I'm sorry, Amanda," she said. "I can't believe what I've just done. But now I can't turn back."

At that moment she noticed that Amanda's arm was thrust upward in an awkward position. It was a stroke of luck, though. She hadn't noticed the wristwatch before. Quickly, she took it off Amanda's wrist and put it on her own. She had less than a half hour to get back to the station. But she couldn't neglect any detail. Everything had to be perfect. One mistake could send her to jail for life.

She pushed the arm back over the torso. Hurrying to the creek, she grabbed two large stones. She returned to the grave and put the stones on the body.

She went back and forth, until she had finally covered the body with rocks. Then she pushed dirt over the rocks to fill in the grave. When the dirt was packed tightly, she spread the brown needles and pine cones to hide the freshly turned earth. No one would see the grave under the deep green branches of the evergreens.

She took a deep breath. She was Amanda MacKenzie now. Stephanie Rendall had disappeared from the face of the earth.

She went back to the creek. Picking up Amanda's purse and the bag containing their uneaten picnic lunch, she took one last look at the area. The bank was clean. There was no trace of what had happened there.

"The hard part is about to begin," she muttered to herself.

Stephanie turned back along the path, retracing their steps. She emerged onto the path alongside the highway and walked briskly toward town. She looked at Amanda's watch. She was running late, and there was still a lot of work to do before she found her way to Cresswell and the unsuspecting family that waited for Amanda MacKenzie.

When Stephanie got back to the Porterville bus station, the bus for Cresswell had already pulled out. But that wasn't her only problem. As she approached the locker where Amanda's luggage was stored, Stephanie realized that she had buried the locker key in the forest. It had been in the pocket of her leather jacket.

"I can't believe it," she muttered to herself. But she knew there was nothing she could do. Going back to the grave site was too horrible to contemplate. "Don't panic," she told herself. "You got yourself this far. Figure it out."

She sat down in a plastic chair that was at the end of a long row of connected seats. Her fingers fumbled with the folds of a bus schedule. She scanned the page. A local bus left for Cresswell in an hour. She had sixty minutes to straighten everything out.

The station was quiet. Stephanie remembered

the location of the locker, and she remembered something that Ted had once taught her. Taking a deep breath, she rifled through Amanda's purse until she found a hairpin. After looking around to make sure no one was watching her, Stephanie began to pick the lock. Sweat poured off her face as she worked.

When the metal door finally flew open, Stephanie let out a sigh of relief. "Thank you, Ted."

He had showed her how to open a public locker. At least she had learned something useful from her former boyfriend.

"One down, one to go."

She removed Amanda's belongings: two suitcases and the canvas tote bag. Her own canvas bag was inside the locker. Moving around the station, she disposed of her possessions in a random fashion, dropping pieces of her clothing in different trash cans. She didn't want them to be found in one lump.

When everything was disposed of properly, she went into the ladies' room. Her hands were still dirty. Using the strong soap from the dispenser, she worked up a heavy lather. As soon as her hands were clean, she stepped back from the mirror and looked at herself.

Then she noticed that there were spots of blood on the dress. It terrified her that she was letting things like this slip by. What if someone had seen the blood? Stephanie changed quickly, putting on slacks and a flannel shirt that she found in the suitcases. Amanda had been a little smaller than Stephanie, and the clothes fit tightly. But she was used to tight-fitting clothes, so it didn't matter. She stuffed the blue dress deep inside the plastic liner of the wastebasket.

Her eyes returned to the mirror. "The hair!"

Though her hair was almost the same color as Amanda's, it was too long. If she wanted to look like Amanda, she had to make it shorter. Hurrying out of the ladies' room, she put the luggage in another locker and took the key. Leaving the station, she moved along the street until she found an open drugstore, where she purchased a pair of cheap scissors.

When she returned to the station, she saw that she had a half-hour before the last bus departed for Cresswell. She had to make it. She didn't want to spend the rest of the night in Porterville, not with Amanda lying buried in Arden Glen.

When she went back into the ladies' room, there were two women in front of the mirrors. Stephanie did not want anyone to see her, so she stepped into a stall. She found a small mirror in Amanda's purse. It would have to do. She began to whack away at her hair, dropping the clippings into the bowl.

She gazed at her new, shorter hair style in the small mirror. "If it's uneven, I can always claim my wicked aunt did this to me."

She left the stall and went back to the large mirrors over the sinks for one more glimpse.

The loudspeaker began to blare in the station. "Attention all passengers. Now arriving at gate one, southbound local bus service to Cresswell, Watertown, Lockly, Reesport—"

Stephanie hurried to the locker and reclaimed the suitcases and the canvas tote. As she was running toward the bus, she saw a uniformed policeman walking through the station, swinging his night stick. Her heart began to pound. She was terrified that he would notice her and see guilt written in all her movements.

But the law officer didn't even look her way. He was heading for the coffee machine at the rear of the station. Stephanie rushed to the bus gate.

Using Amanda's ticket, she boarded the motorcoach. She put the suitcases in the overhead rack and then set the tote bag next to her on the empty seat. Immediately, she began to rifle through Amanda's purse. She counted the Canadian money, which was tinted with different colors. Amanda had left her almost a hundred Canadian dollars. Stephanie wasn't sure how that would translate to American funds, but she knew she would need all of the colorful currency.

As the bus pulled out of Porterville, Stephanie began eating one of the sandwiches and continued to pore through Amanda's purse. The pink envelopes were still there. She knew she had to read Elizabeth's letters before she got to Cresswell. The bus ride would take less than an hour. She had to read quickly.

Chapter 7

When Elizabeth walked through the front door of her house, she slammed the door a little too hard. The noise brought her mother from the kitchen. Nina Henley immediately noticed the distraught look on her daughter's face. Elizabeth slammed her purse on the table in the foyer.

"Honey, what's wrong?"

"It's Amanda," Elizabeth replied worriedly. "She wasn't on the second bus, Mom. Something has happened to her. I just know it."

Mrs. Henley moved toward her daughter. "We should call her aunt and uncle right away," she said.

Elizabeth drew back, turning away from her mother. She knew she couldn't call Amanda's home in New Brunswick. Any attempt to contact her guardians would result in disaster. Her aunt and uncle would know where Amanda had gone. Their plot would be discovered.

"I think they're away this week," Elizabeth

lied. "Amanda said they were going to take a vacation after she left."

"We should still try," Mrs. Henley replied. "Do you have her number in New Brunswick?"

"No," Elizabeth said quickly. "We never exchanged numbers. It was long distance, so her aunt and uncle wouldn't let her call. And I thought you and Dad would get angry if I ran up a big phone bill. We just wrote letters."

Mrs. Henley started for the living room. "Well, this is an emergency and I want to find out what's going on. I'll call the operator for the area code for New Brunswick. Grand Bay, isn't it?"

"No, Mom!"

"What, dear?"

"I mean, let me do it. I feel responsible."

Mrs. Henley smiled. "Sure, honey. If it makes you feel better."

Moving into the living room, Elizabeth picked up the phone and dialed local directory assistance. She asked for the area code for New Brunswick. The operator gave her the code and told her that it would no problem to dial direct.

Elizabeth was going to pretend to call New Brunswick. She hated to lie to her mother, but it was necessary if she was going to continue the deception. If Amanda's aunt and uncle found out where she had gone, they might try to come after her. Elizabeth and Amanda would both be in deep trouble.

She was pretending to make her call when a knock resounded on the front door. Running to the door, she threw it open only to see her father standing in the threshold.

"Hi, Liz," George Henley said. "Is Amanda here yet?"

Elizabeth shook her head. "Not yet. Two buses came in but she wasn't on either one of them."

George Henley frowned. He was a round, sweet-faced, gray-haired man of fifty. His business, Henley's Hardware, was a fixture on Warren Street in Cresswell.

"I'm worried about her," Elizabeth said.

Mr. Henley had a no-nonsense way of expressing himself. "Get on the horn, honey. Find out what's going on."

"I was just getting ready to call New Brunswick," Elizabeth said hesitantly. She averted her brown eyes. Elizabeth had never been able to lie to her father. He had a way of looking right through her.

"No word from her at all?" he asked his daughter.

"Well, there was a message after the first bus came in," she replied. "Amanda was supposed to be on the next bus, but she never showed up."

Mr. Henley rubbed his chin. "Doesn't sound

too serious. Maybe she just missed the second bus. Got off to sightsee and lost track of the time. Was there another bus tonight?"

Elizabeth shrugged. "I didn't think to check."

He looked at his watch. "It's almost seven now. Well, get going, Liz. Make your calls. Check with the bus station. Call Amanda's folks. If we can't locate her, we can get the sheriff in on it."

"The sheriff?" Elizabeth muttered.

Mr. Henley put his arm around her shoulder. "It's okay, Liz. I'm sure Amanda is all right. But there's a way of doing things in a situation like this. Now go make your calls."

"Okay, Dad. You're right."

To stall for time, she called the Cresswell bus station first. Another southbound bus had come in, but no one was sure if Amanda had been on it. Even after Elizabeth described her, the ticket agent still drew a blank.

"Any luck?" her father asked.

"No."

"Call Canada," he replied. "You've got to check it out."

For a moment, Elizabeth wondered if she should tell her father the truth. But she decided that the truth could wait. If Amanda had been delayed for some other reason, there was no sense in telling all she knew right now. Of course, if she had to come clean, maybe with the

46

sheriff, she would do so without hesitation. But until then, she would protect their secret.

Dialing directory assistance in New Brunswick, she asked for the number of Amanda's aunt and uncle. After writing down the number, she pretended to call Grand Bay. She really dialed the toll-free number for the state weather information service.

"No answer," she told her father. "Amanda did say they were taking a vacation after she left."

Mr. Henley moved toward the phone. "Here, let me try. You might have dialed it wrong."

"I called the right number, Dad."

"Better safe than sorry."

Mrs. Henley stuck her head out of the kitchen. "Any luck yet?"

"No," Elizabeth replied. She felt a nervous tingle spreading through her body. If her father got through, the whole scheme would be revealed. Her parents would know that she had lied. They would be so disappointed in her.

"Dad, maybe we—"

Mr. Henley turned back toward the front door. "Maybe that's her now."

The rapping sounded on the door again. Elizabeth ran out of the living room. She tore open the door.

Her eyes grew wide when she saw the smiling

girl standing in the threshold. "Amanda! It's you, it's really you."

"I made it!"

Stephanie Rendall stepped into the Henley home. Elizabeth embraced her. She had made it just in time. Everything was going to be all right.

A half-hour later, they were sitting around the dinner table in the Henleys' dining room. Stephanie was nervous. Her stomach felt tight, but she still had to appear to be enjoying the meal.

Elizabeth smiled across the table, winking at her. "Oh, I can't believe you're here. We were so worried about you."

"I told you she got off the bus to sightsee," Mr. Henley said boisterously.

Stephanie swallowed and tried to smile warmly. "I have a confession to make. I got off in Porterville by mistake. I was half asleep when the bus pulled in there. I was so anxious to get to Cresswell that I must have heard the driver wrong. It was a stupid mistake."

"Well, you're here now," Elizabeth said effusively.

Mrs. Henley gazed straight at her. "What did you see while you were in Porterville, Amanda?"

Stephanie's face went slack. It was a trick question. They were trying to trip her up, force her into making a mistake.

"I just walked around town," Stephanie said, shrugging, as if what she had done was of no importance. "I was going to get my money changed, but the banks I went to didn't handle currency exchange."

"How did you pay the cab driver?" Mr. Henley asked.

"Oh, I had a few American dollars that I got last year," Stephanie said quickly. "I've been keeping them in my top drawer for inspiration. I didn't want to forget that someday I'd be coming to Cresswell." She hoped that she sounded sufficiently industrious, with just the right amount of naiveté for them to feel comfortable with her in their house. After all, this was what she wanted, a fresh start in life with a nice family in a beautiful home. She had killed for this. But all the bad things were behind her now. She was going to live a good life and make something of herself.

Mr. Henley nodded and went back to his plate of spaghetti.

"You can change your money tomorrow," Elizabeth said. "I'll drive you to my bank. I've got my own car."

Stephanie recalled one of Elizabeth's letters. "I know. A Ford Escort. Your father bought it for your birthday."

"Do you have a car in New Brunswick?" Mr. Henley asked.

Another trick question. "No, I don't," she answered.

A pearl of sweat trickled down the side of Stephanie's smooth face. She wiped it away with her dinner napkin. The pressure was on. And it was going to get worse. They were not going to stop asking her questions. She had to *be* Amanda MacKenzie. She had to be careful so she would not get caught in a mistake.

"More spaghetti, Amanda?" Mrs. Henley asked.

"No thank you."

She tried to be polite and demure, just like Amanda. She had to be convincing if she was going to pull it off. She had to stay in character. It was harder than she had figured. She hoped she had not made a mistake coming to Cresswell as Amanda MacKenzie. Stephanie knew she could always run if it got too hot.

"Mr. and Mrs. Henley, may I say something?"

"Certainly," Mrs. Henley replied.

Mr. Henley looked straight at her. "Go right ahead, Amanda."

Stephanie took a deep breath. "I want to thank you for taking me into your home. It's the nicest thing anyone has ever done for me. I—I don't know if Elizabeth has told you, but my aunt and uncle aren't very warm people. I really don't think they wanted me after my parents were killed."

Elizabeth grimaced. "Amanda!"

"Your mother and father should know," Stephanie said. It was a gamble but she knew that a small heartfelt revelation would evoke sympathy and help cover up for the times when her answers would be terse for fear that she would say the wrong thing. "I'm not used to such hospitality. I can see right away what a nice home this is, and I'm so grateful to be here."

George and Nina Henley were both gazing sympathetically at the blue-eyed girl across the table from them. Stephanie knew by their caring expressions that she had them. They were straight out of some fantasy television family. The Henleys could be fooled, but Stephanie knew she had to be careful every moment.

"Well," Mrs. Henley said, "we're glad to have you."

"Yes," Mr. Henley told her. "If you need anything, you just ask."

"Thank you," Stephanie said, smiling at each of them in turn. "Thank you so much."

"By the way," Mr. Henley said, "don't you think you should call your aunt and uncle to tell them you made it here all right?"

Stephanie tensed, ready to dodge another question. "I already did," she replied quickly. "I called them from Porterville while I was waiting."

"I thought they were on vacation," Mrs. Henley said. "That's what Elizabeth told us."

Stephanie felt herself turn red. Why were they so quick to find flaws in her story?

"Yes, they are away," she said. "I called them at their hotel. They weren't in, but I left a message. Everything is fine."

She noticed Elizabeth smiling at her. She seemed so nice and accepting.

Elizabeth pushed away from the table. "May we be excused?" she asked. "I want to show Amanda around."

"Go right ahead," Mrs. Henley said. "I'm sure you girls have a lot to talk about."

Elizabeth got up. "Come on, Amanda. I'll show you your room."

Stephanie rose from her seat at the same time. "Thank you. The dinner was great."

Chapter 8

"This is it," Elizabeth said, making a wide gesture around the third-story bedroom. "It's all yours, Amanda. What do you think?"

Stephanie surveyed the bright chamber. Red-and-blue flowered paper gave the walls a distinctive New England look, as if the figures had been laboriously stenciled on the surface. A sloping ceiling marked one side of the room. It tapered down to a three-foot section of wall above the floor.

"You'll have to be careful not to bump your head," Elizabeth told her. "Well?"

Stephanie began to cry. Though it appeared to Elizabeth that her new visitor was overcome by the generosity of the Henley family, Stephanie was actually letting go of the tensions and conflicting emotions that had built up inside her.

Elizabeth put a comforting hand on her shoulder. "Hey, it's okay. You're like one of the family now."

Stephanie tried to smile through the tears.

"I'm sorry. It's just—I don't know. I never thought I'd make it. But here I am."

Elizabeth smiled warmly. "Wow, that was a close call at dinner. For a minute I thought you were going to tell Mom and Dad that you had run away from New Brunswick."

Stephanie dried her eyes. "No, I'm not that crazy. But I wanted to be honest about my aunt and uncle. That way, nobody will be surprised when they don't write or check up on me." *And you and your parents will keep feeling sorry for me,* she thought.

"Good thinking," Elizabeth replied. "Well, I'm waiting. I decorated your room myself. How do you like it?"

Stephanie turned, taking a closer look. A single bed rested along the far wall, next to the window. The bed was covered by a lacy white comforter. There was a wooden nightstand next to the bed. A small oak desk, a wooden chair, and a mirrored dresser finished off the decor.

"It's beautiful," Stephanie said. "Better than my room in Grand Bay."

"I'm so happy you like it," Elizabeth replied. "By the way, what happened to your hair?"

Stephanie tried to act nonchalant. "I don't know what you mean."

"Your haircut," Elizabeth said. "I don't want to criticize, but it's uneven. Who did that to you?"

Stephanie had already made up her story. "My aunt," she said with a disgusted sigh. "She didn't want to pay for a stylist."

Elizabeth fingered the ragged ends of Stephanie's hair. "I think I can fix it. Here, sit down."

She pulled the chair away from the desk. "Wait here. I'll get some scissors and a comb," she said as she disappeared into the hallway.

Stephanie sat down, feeling satisfied with her performance. She thought that possibly she could like Elizabeth.

"All set, Amanda." Elizabeth raced back into the room.

"Are you sure about this, Elizabeth? I mean, the mess will—"

Elizabeth stomped on the floor. "Hardwood. We'll sweep it up with no trouble. Now hold still."

Elizabeth went to work on Stephanie's hair. "Your aunt really butchered you," she exclaimed.

"She's so cheap," Stephanie scoffed.

Elizabeth continued to snip for another ten minutes. "There. Take a look. It's a lot better now."

Stephanie stood up. She looked at herself in the mirror on the dresser. Her face went slack. For a moment, she saw Amanda's face staring back at her.

Elizabeth frowned. "What's wrong? I didn't mess it up, did I?"

Stephanie blinked and her own countenance came into focus. "No, it—it looks great. Thank you."

Elizabeth looked at the floor. "Better sweep up before Mom has a fit. She likes to keep things neat. I'll get the broom."

Stephanie continued to stare at herself. She had not really seen Amanda's face, she told herself. The light was strange. It had been a momentary illusion.

When the hair clippings were swept up and disposed of, Elizabeth closed the bedroom door. She turned the key in the lock. Stephanie's eyes narrowed. She wondered why Elizabeth was acting so secretive.

"Elizabeth, what are you—"

Elizabeth's nose wrinkled. "Sorry about the secret-agent routine. But I wanted to ask you about your records."

"Records? I don't have a—"

"School records," Elizabeth said. "Did you bring them with you?"

Stephanie frowned. "I—"

"Remember? We agreed it would be best if you brought your school records with you. That way Cresswell High won't have to contact your old school in Grand Bay. They won't try to get in touch with your aunt and uncle."

Amanda hadn't mentioned a thing about records on the bus. Again Stephanie had to think quickly. She had to cover herself either way. She wished she had had time to go through everything in Amanda's suitcases. She had wasted too much time on the letters.

"Oh no," she said with a worried expression on her face. "I hope I remembered to pack them. I'd better look now. Elizabeth, what are we going to do if I left them in Grand Bay?"

"Let's worry about that later. Check your bags."

"I left in such a hurry," Stephanie intoned. "And it was dark. I had everything ready, but I was so nervous."

"Sure, I understand."

Stephanie began to unpack the first suitcase. Elizabeth helped her by putting away the clothes in the dresser as Stephanie took them from the bags. The transcripts were not in the first suitcase.

"I hope I didn't forget them," Stephanie said. "It could ruin everything." *And get me thrown in jail.*

"Keep looking," Elizabeth urged.

As Stephanie unpacked the second suitcase, she tossed a gold charm bracelet on the bed. It bore charms in many different shapes. It was not the kind of jewelry that Stephanie would have bought for herself.

Elizabeth picked up the bracelet. "Wow."

Stephanie grimaced. "That tacky thing. You can have it if you want it. I never wear it anymore."

A hurt expression spread over Elizabeth's face. "Amanda, I gave this to you. You saw it in a catalogue. I sent it to you for your birthday because you said you wanted one."

Stephanie smiled, even though her gut was churning from the mistake she had made. "I was just kidding, you silly person. I wouldn't part with that bracelet for anything. You know how much I love it."

"Oh," Elizabeth said hesitantly. "I'm sorry. I don't mean to be overly sensitive."

But Stephanie could see that Elizabeth wasn't really amused. She was straightforward, and she took things seriously, and Stephanie had to keep that in mind. She also had to watch what she said. She knew that her glib comment about the bracelet had been a potentially fatal mistake.

Stephanie picked up the bracelet, put it on, and lifted it into the light. "Beautiful. I can't thank you enough, Elizabeth. It was the best birthday present I ever got."

Elizabeth gestured toward the open suitcase. "You'd better keep looking for those transcripts."

Stephanie dug into the suitcase again. Suddenly her hands felt a large envelope. She opened it, praying that the right papers were in there. She found transcripts with the official seal of Grand Bay High School. "Here," she said. "I found it."

Amanda had been a good student. Her grades were excellent, another obstacle for Stephanie to overcome.

She handed the papers to Elizabeth. "Will this be enough?"

Elizabeth studied the transcripts. "Great. Oh, this will be perfect, Amanda. I can get my friend in the office to fix everything. We're home free."

"I hope so," Stephanie replied. "I really hope so."

Chapter 9

Elizabeth left the third-floor bedroom after her guest said that she was tired. After she said good night and left the room, Elizabeth heard the key turning in the lock. She hurried down the stairs to her own bedroom on the second floor.

The bright, cozy chamber had a double bed, a dresser, a desk and chair, and a nightstand. It was a lot like Amanda's room, since Elizabeth had decorated both of them. Elizabeth changed into her pajamas and fell onto her bed. She grabbed Mr. Monkton, a stuffed gorilla that she had received on her sixth birthday. It was the only childhood toy that hadn't been put away in the attic.

Elizabeth always held Mr. Monkton when she was angry or in a state of distress. Something didn't seem right. Amanda was safe and sound in Cresswell, but Elizabeth no longer felt the elation that had come with her arrival. She was filled with a strange, nagging sense of dread.

Amanda's comment about the bracelet had hurt Elizabeth. The offhand remark had not seemed like a joke. Amanda had tried to smooth it over but the incident had left Elizabeth with a bad taste in her mouth.

Thinking back, Elizabeth tried to remember if Amanda's letters had ever been cruel or flippant. But Amanda had always seemed sweet, innocent, and sensitive. Except for her complaints about her guardians, Amanda had never written a bad word about anyone. She had never revealed anything that would indicate she had a mean aspect to her nature.

Elizabeth sighed. She knew she had to put things in perspective. Amanda had to be scared. She had run away from a bad situation. She was in a new town, in a foreign country in fact. Amanda had a right to be confused, rattled. She would come around when she got used to life in Cresswell.

Clutching Mr. Monkton tightly to her chest, Elizabeth closed her eyes and told herself that everything was going to be all right. She just had to give Amanda a chance. The sweetness would come out sooner or later. Elizabeth was sure of it.

Stephanie lay back on her soft bed, looking up at the flowery wallpaper. She was free of her

parents and free of Ted. She had a new family—
a new past, even.

"It looks like your luck has turned, girl," she
muttered to herself.

Despite her success, Stephanie still had plenty
of things to worry about. She cringed at the mistake she had made with the charm bracelet. She
knew she had to be Elizabeth's friend. She had
to be closer to her than any of her other friends
were. Elizabeth was her key to survival.

But Elizabeth was just the kind of goody-
goody that Stephanie had always loathed. Elizabeth was great in school, and she was perky and
effusive. She had all the energy of a well-ad-
justed teenager, something that Stephanie had
never possessed. But it was no time to be cynical.
She wanted to have Elizabeth's qualities. She
wanted to be perky and effusive. She had to *be*
the innocent female that had written those pen-
pal letters. And she had every reason to be, now
that she was beginning her new life.

She closed her eyes for a moment. Suddenly
she sat up in bed. She had heard something. A
low moaning sound had reached her ears. For a
moment, she imagined that it was Amanda, crying from her grave along the bank of the brook.

But when she listened closely, she realized
that it was only the rafters of the house, creaking
in the brisk wind that blew over Cresswell.

Chapter 10

"Here we are," Elizabeth said sweetly. "Cresswell High. What do you think, Amanda?"

As they rolled into the senior parking lot in Elizabeth's Escort, Stephanie gazed toward the imposing brick building. For nearly a week, Stephanie had been preparing to attend school again. Elizabeth had taken her shopping for school supplies—paper, notebooks, pens and pencils. Stephanie's cash reserve had not been large enough for her to afford new school clothes, so Elizabeth had been kind enough to give her some of her old things.

But nothing could have readied Stephanie for the dread of facing the first day at a new school. She was suddenly filled with terror. The reality of her assumed identity had finally come home in a big way. Fooling the Henleys had been easy, but this was a whole school full of people, always asking questions, always curious.

Elizabeth pulled her car into a parking space. "I can't wait to introduce you to everyone. Amanda?"

Stephanie didn't reply. She felt lightheaded. Her face had turned pale. Small beads of sweat were popping out on her forehead. She was beginning to wonder if she could go through with the charade.

"It's going to be all right," Elizabeth said, offering a comforting tap on Stephanie's arm.

Stephanie shook her head. "What if something goes wrong?" She held up the transcripts. *And I end up in jail!*

Elizabeth smiled reassuringly. "Nothing will go wrong. Don't worry."

"But what if all my credits aren't accepted?" She didn't want to be held back or have to take special courses and be noticed any more than she had to be.

"Don't worry," Elizabeth replied. "I studied your transcripts. You have more than enough credits for your senior year. You'll be able to take four electives. The only required subjects are English and civics. You can sign up for classes that you like, take anything you want. It'll be easy. You're smart."

Amanda had been smart. Stephanie trembled at the thought of trying to live up to Amanda's good-girl reputation. But she had to get a grip on herself; otherwise Elizabeth would become suspicious.

Elizabeth frowned at her. "Are you sure you're all right, Amanda?"

Stephanie sighed and nodded. "Stage fright. I mean, it's my first day and all. I guess it's finally sinking in that I've left my aunt and uncle."

They climbed out of Elizabeth's car and started for the entrance of Cresswell High. Students were buzzing around, getting acquainted before the first bell rang and ended their summer freedom. As Elizabeth and Stephanie approached the front steps, a group of boys turned to look at them.

A playful smile stretched over Elizabeth's mouth. "Here it comes, Amanda. Just what you've been waiting for. Boys."

Stephanie smirked at the expectant faces of the boys. She wasn't really looking forward to dealing with immature high-school guys. After going out with Ted, they would seem boring. But Amanda hadn't dated in her whole life, so Stephanie had to act enthusiastic.

A tall, dark-haired boy winked at them. "Hi, Elizabeth. Who's your friend?" He looked at Stephanie and extended his hand. "Haven't seen you before."

Elizabeth grimaced at the boy. "Her name is Amanda MacKenzie. Amanda, this is Richard Tibbs."

They shook hands. Stephanie tried to affect a pleased but demure attitude. "It's nice to meet you, Richard. But we have to hurry. I'm not registered yet."

"Maybe I'll see you in one of my classes," Richard said hopefully.

Elizabeth rolled her eyes and grabbed Stephanie's arm. "She's busy now, Richard."

They started up the steps.

"He's kind of cute," Stephanie said. She knew Amanda would have thought so. Actually, she thought so herself. He had brown wavy hair, a pleasant smile, and a nice build.

"There's worse," Elizabeth said, guiding her up the front steps. "Let's get you registered and then we can worry about dating."

"Do you have a boyfriend?" Stephanie asked.

"I did. His name was Scott, remember? Didn't I tell you about how he started seeing someone else?"

Stephanie just nodded. She had read about Scott in the pink letters, but she hadn't really remembered him. She had actually grown tired of scanning the chatty correspondence. But it was her only link to the girl who lay moldering in Porterville's Arden Glen.

They went through the front door and turned right down the corridor. Elizabeth led Stephanie to a glass door marked Office. Stephanie began to worry again. She had to get through the paperwork before the ruse could go on. One technicality could sink her.

Elizabeth stopped her by the glass door. "Quick, give me your transcripts."

"What?"

"Give them to me and wait here."

"Why?" Stephanie asked.

"Because," Elizabeth replied, "my friend Trudy works in the office. I'll run this stuff by her and see what I can do."

"Okay, if you think that's best. Good luck, Elizabeth."

"Sure." She started to open the door.

"Wait," Stephanie said.

"Yes?"

Stephanie took a deep breath. "Elizabeth, if things don't work out, I'll take all the blame. There's no need to get you in trouble." It was the kind of thing Amanda would have said.

Elizabeth winked at her. "We'll worry about that if it happens. Give me a minute. I'll call you when we're ready." Elizabeth went into the office.

Stephanie leaned back against the wall. She considered her options. If the scheme went sour, she could run, take another bus out of Cresswell. She could always tell the Henlcys that she was going back to New Brunswick. They wouldn't be any wiser to her. By the time someone figured out what had happened, Stephanie could be all the way to Florida or California.

A hand fell on her shoulder. Stephanie flinched. She shrugged away from the hand,

69

turning to look at Richard Tibbs. He had followed her into the building.

"Hi, stranger. I didn't mean to startle you," he
said.

His manner was that of an impetuous, awkward boy. Stephanie figured she could handle
him, especially since Elizabeth was not there to
watch.

Richard leaned closer to her. "You're Elizabeth's pen-pal friend, aren't you?"

Stephanie eyed him carefully. "That's right,"
she answered.

"How about if I call you sometime so I can
show you around?"

Stephanie didn't like the way he was breathing down her neck. She looked toward the office
door to make sure Elizabeth wasn't coming
back. "Look, junior," she snapped, "why don't
you go find yourself a nice sophomore who
hasn't heard your line of bull yet, okay? Or do
you want to be singing soprano in the glee
club?"

Richard looked stunned. It was clear that he
hadn't expected the innocent-looking girl to talk
to him in such a harsh manner. But before he
could say something, the office door opened.

Elizabeth reached out to grab Stephanie's
arm. "Okay, Amanda. All set. We're ready for
you."

Stephanie didn't look back at Richard as she followed Elizabeth into the school office.

Elizabeth's friend Trudy was sitting behind a desk. She was a green-eyed girl with short-cropped black hair. Thick glasses covered her plain face. Trudy was looking over the transcripts from Grand Bay. When she glanced up, she smiled at Stephanie, revealing her silver braces.

"Hi," Stephanie said meekly.

Trudy gestured to the transcripts. "You're a good student, Amanda."

"Thanks," Stephanie replied.

Trudy winked at her. "I don't think there's going to be any problem. I've got all the papers filled out. And here comes the assistant principal now. All Mr. Lipton has to do is sign these papers and you're an official student at Cresswell, Amanda."

Stephanie turned to see a stern-faced man entering through the glass door. Henry Lipton looked like an assistant principal. He had sharp, scrutinizing eyes and a crew cut. Stephanie flinched when he glared at her.

"What seems to be the problem?" Mr. Lipton asked.

Elizabeth and Stephanie both tensed. The moment of truth had arrived. The whole plan depended on Lipton's reaction.

"No problem," Trudy replied. "Just a transfer

student, Mr. Lipton. I've got all the papers filled out. All you have to do is sign them."

Mr. Lipton took the papers from Trudy's hand. His hawkish eyes scanned the transcripts and the application forms. After a moment, he looked up at Stephanie.

"You're Amanda MacKenzie?" Mr. Lipton asked accusingly, as if he expected her to say no.

Stephanie nodded. "Yes, sir."

Mr. Lipton squinted at the transcripts and then at her. "How'd you end up in Cresswell from Canada, Miss MacKenzie?"

"She's my cousin," Elizabeth said quickly. "She's staying with my family."

"Oh," Mr. Lipton replied. "Well, you're in good hands, Amanda." He looked at the transcripts one more time, which made Stephanie freeze to the bone. "Well," he went on, "it looks like you're a good student, Amanda. Is her schedule ready yet, Trudy?"

Trudy nodded. "All set."

He grabbed a pen from the desk and signed the transfer papers. "Welcome to Cresswell High, Amanda. If you have any problems, feel free to knock on my door. I'm always willing to listen."

Stephanie smiled. "Thank you, sir. Thank you very much."

* * *

Elizabeth was anxious to talk to Amanda. She had not seen her pen pal since she walked her to her first period class, civics. She hoped Amanda had gotten through her first day without any trouble. She would find out in English, the only subject they had together. They had both ended up in Mr. Fern's sixth-period honors class.

"Hey, Elizabeth."

Richard Tibbs walked up beside her.

"Hi, Richard. How are you?"

Richard shook his head. "Your friend Amanda almost took my head off this morning."

Elizabeth frowned, looking at him. "What?"

"Yeah. She threatened to make my life a little shorter just because I asked her to go out."

"I can't believe it, Richard. Are you sure you didn't misunderstand her?"

"Hardly," Richard exclaimed. "She's not as nice as you made her out to be." He drifted away when Elizabeth didn't say anything.

She kept walking toward English class. She couldn't believe that Amanda had been mean to Richard, even if he had been over zealous, even obnoxious, in his approach.

Still, the uneasy feeling came back to her. Something seemed out of kilter. When she reached the room for Mr. Fern's honors class, she stopped by the door, waiting for Amanda to come down the hall.

Chapter 11

Stephanie ambled down the hall, heading for English class. So far the school day had been a breeze. Stephanie was beginning to feel good about the switch she had made with the girl in Arden Glen. She could graduate as Amanda and go on to live her entire life as the nice girl from Canada, maybe even go to college or find a good job.

Her first-period class had been civics. The teacher was Mrs. Mobley, a kind-hearted older woman who seemed interested in the fact that "Amanda" was from New Brunswick. Perhaps over the course of the semester, the teacher had suggested, Amanda would tell the class about the Canadian governmental and judicial system. Stephanie nodded politely, at the offer, while her whole body tingled with fear.

Second period was a class called Modern Media. The focus was on American newspapers, magazines, movies, and television. Stephanie figured it was no big deal. She could read newspapers and magazines. She could watch movies and television. It was a cakewalk.

Third period brought creative writing. Stephanie had always enjoyed reading, and at one time, a few years ago, she used to write stories. Another cakewalk.

Study hall came during fourth period, right before lunch, and so Stephanie had an hour-and-a-half break in the middle of the day. She could read or do her homework. She had time to herself to prepare for the rest of the day.

Fifth period was art class, her favorite of the day. Drawing, painting, and ceramics were the focus. The teacher was Mr. Davenport, a cheerful young man who was nice and sort of flirty. He had really seemed to like Stephanie. She saw herself getting an A from Mr. Davenport.

She had no idea that trouble would rear its head in Mr. Fern's sixth-period honors English class.

Elizabeth glanced up the hallway, watching for Amanda. She didn't want her friend to be late. Mr. Fern could be picky and strict about tardiness. He had a reputation for being a real pain.

As she waited, Elizabeth kept thinking of what Richard had said about Amanda. He had insisted that Amanda was nasty, almost vulgar to him. Ordinarily, Elizabeth would have written off Richard as a jerk. But she still remembered the stinging remark Amanda had made about the charm bracelet that Elizabeth had given her. She tried to push back her doubts, but they were still there in her mind.

She finally saw her new friend coming down the hall toward her. Elizabeth waved and Amanda waved back, grinning broadly as she sauntered up to her.

"Hi, Elizabeth."

Elizabeth studied her face. "You look happy."

"I am. It's been a good day."

"Amanda, Richard tried to tell me that you gave him a really hard time this morning."

"No, not really," Amanda replied pleasantly. "I mean, he was bothering me while I waited outside the office. I think it's a little too early for him to be asking if he can call me. I politely asked him to leave me alone. That was all."

Elizabeth nodded, satisfied that Richard had been exaggerating. "Honestly, he can be such a jerk."

"Yes, I'm finding that out," agreed Amanda, with a prim, self-satisfied smile on her face.

The tardy bell rang. Elizabeth urged her friend into the classroom. They hurried to their desks, sitting next to each other. When they glanced up, they saw Mr. Fern glaring at them.

"Well," he said coldly, "so glad you could

make it. Now, if you'll open your notebooks, we can begin the lesson."

Mr. Fern paced back and forth in front of the class. He was an alarmingly thin man with short-cropped hair and thick glasses that made him appear bug-eyed.

"This is honors English," he droned. "College-preparatory English, not some kindergarten class. We're going to study many things, including the difference between denotative and connotative writing. This knowledge will be imperative to anyone entering college. So, do any of you seniors have a clue as to what these forms of writing entail?"

The whole class was frozen. They feared Mr. Fern. No one wanted to answer his question incorrectly and face his sarcasm.

His protuberant eyes surveyed the class. "Well, since none of you heroes wants to volunteer, I'll have to choose a volunteer. You there—"

He pointed right at Stephanie. She blushed. She had not expected to be singled out from the others.

"What is your name?" Mr. Fern asked.

"Amanda, Amanda MacKenzie."

He picked up his class roll. "Why don't I find your name on my list?"

"She just transferred here from New Brunswick," Elizabeth said, speaking up for her friend. "She—"

Mr. Fern glared at Elizabeth. "I wasn't talking to you. Miss MacKenzie, when you were in New Brunswick, did you happen to study the difference between denotative and connotative writing?"

Stephanie tried to look right into his weird eyes. "No, sir."

"Well, then, perhaps you'd like to venture a guess. After all, you saw fit to come into my class after the bell rang. Surely you must be ahead of the rest of the class if you're taking such liberties on the first day of school. Why don't you answer my question?"

Stephanie's teeth were grinding. She couldn't believe she was being put on the spot in such a way.

"No comment?" Mr. Fern said. "Well, perhaps when you write home to your friends in New Brunswick, you can tell them that your chances of being a college graduate in America are slim, very slim." He turned away from the class for a moment.

"You jerk," Stephanie muttered under her breath.

"I beg your pardon?" Mr. Fern asked, wheeling toward the class. "Who said that?"

Elizabeth raised her hand. "I said, could you

write it on the board? I'd like to know the answer, Mr. Fern."

He made a snotty sound. "Well, at least someone has displayed a sense of curiosity. Listen, Miss MacKenzie, and perhaps you'll learn something."

He turned away again, lifting a piece of chalk. "Now, the main difference between denotative and connotative writing . . ."

Stephanie watched him, totally humiliated. But most of all she was angry that she had allowed herself to step outside Amanda's character. The normal tribulations of daily life were making her revert to being the sarcastic, temperamental girl that she was. It was a struggle being Amanda, but she knew she had to keep trying. Little did she know that, before going home to the warmth and comfort of the Henley household, her resolve would be tested to the breaking point.

After the last class, Stephanie went to her locker before meeting Elizabeth out at the parking lot. From out of nowhere, it seemed, Richard materialized over her shoulder.

"I heard you told off Mr. Fern today," he announced enthusiastically. "That was great."

She turned and stared at him. It frightened her that he should stalk her like this.

"I didn't tell off anybody," she said calmly. "I don't know what you're talking about."

She shut her locker and started down the corridor. Richard was not to be deterred. He walked along beside her.

"It's all over school. You called Mr. Fern a jerk."

She stopped and looked him in the eye. "Listen, I don't understand why you're so interested in what I do. But I'd appreciate it if I could attend my classes without being harassed." Stephanie was conscious of avoiding sarcasm and affecting a tone of polite indignation. She was Amanda. She had to remember that.

Richard stepped back and looked chagrined. "I'm sorry I've seemed pushy," he said. "I've been looking forward to seeing you ever since Elizabeth told me about you. You seemed so genuine. I've liked you ever since I heard about you."

Gently she placed her hand on his forearm. "That's very nice, Richard. But I'm new here. My studies are important to me. You have to give me a chance to get adjusted. So please don't chase after me anymore."

With that, she turned and started down the corridor again. For a moment, Richard stood where he was and stared at her. Then, as if suddenly infused with new inspiration, he raced after her once again. He caught up with her at the door leading to the parking lot.

"There's something strange about you, Amanda," he announced. "There's something very strange, and I'm going to figure out what it is."

Stephanie didn't turn around. She pushed open the door and let it slam in Richard's face as a cold chill of fear gripped her body.

"How was school today?" Mr. Henley asked.

They were all sitting at the dinner table. Elizabeth tensed when her father asked the question. She had tried to talk to Amanda about the incident in class, but Amanda seemed to feel it was old news and not worthy of discussion. She couldn't understand Amanda's temper. Was this the same girl who had written her such lovely, sensitive letters?

"It was fine," Amanda said.

"Mr. Fern picked on Amanda," Elizabeth said. She thought that if she brought up the subject in front of her parents, Amanda would be forced to reveal her feelings.

Amanda shrugged. "Oh, he's not so bad. He just caught me off guard. He seems like the kind of teacher who can challenge his students."

Elizabeth looked sideways at her. "He was really mean to you, Amanda. He didn't have to do that."

"He was mean to everyone," Amanda replied. "I don't take it personally."

"You sure are forgiving," said Elizabeth.

Amanda smiled. "It's easy to be that way when I'm living with such nice people."

Mrs. Henley smiled slightly. "Well, I hope you girls are all right in Mr. Fern's class. He sounds like a stinker."

Elizabeth wasn't really concerned about Mr. Fern's honors English class. She had had teachers like him before, and she was confident that she would do well. What concerned her was her houseguest. She was going to reread all of Amanda's letters. Maybe then she could figure out this strange person who was living with her.

Chapter 12

"Hi, Elizabeth," Trudy said. "Where's Amanda?"

Elizabeth turned in the hallway, grimacing at Trudy. "I don't know where she is. I haven't seen her since this morning."

Trudy moved beside her, accompanying Elizabeth down the hall. "Well," she went on, "we need more volunteers to help with the decorations for the homecoming dance. Are you going to ask Amanda to be on the committee?"

Elizabeth sighed. It was only the end of September, but Amanda had already become popular with the other members of the senior class. Everyone seemed to know Amanda, though no one, not even Elizabeth, could say they were really close to her.

"I talked to Amanda yesterday in creative writing," Trudy said when she didn't get an immediate answer. "She said she was interested in being on the committee as long as it was all right with you."

"Sure," Elizabeth replied blankly. "If she wants to help, that's fine. The dance isn't for another two weeks."

Trudy shrugged. "I know. But we should go ahead and get started. We have to buy all the decorations. And before we can do that, we have to submit a price list to the student council so we can get the money."

Elizabeth glared at Trudy. "I'm aware of that. I *am* the chairperson of the committee. I've got it under control."

A hurt expression had formed on Trudy's smooth face. "Well, *excuse* me. I'm sorry I bothered you." She stomped off down the hall.

"Trudy!"

Elizabeth suddenly felt horrible about the way she had acted. She shouldn't have snapped at Trudy. She continued on to her fourth-period Spanish class. She had been in a foul mood for more than a week.

As she plopped down at her station in the language lab, Elizabeth analyzed the reasons for her snit. The semester had not gone exactly the way she had envisioned it at the beginning of the school year. She hadn't been re-elected to the student council. And Scott Johnson, who had been so nice last spring, had met Patricia Hendricks over the summer, and now they were an item. Although there was nothing wrong with having a productive senior year and getting into a good college, Elizabeth had hoped that she would have an active social life.

But these disappointments were not the real cause of her anxieties. When she was truthful with herself, one reason came to mind— Amanda MacKenzie.

Elizabeth's relationship with Amanda had not blossomed at all, not in the way that she had hoped. They rode to school every morning in Elizabeth's Escort and then went home together at the end of the day. They sat together at breakfast and at dinner, where Amanda was always polite and courteous. Amanda even helped with the household chores.

But they hadn't become close in the way that Amanda's letters had suggested that they would. There was no confiding, no girl talk beyond the usual surface conversation. Whenever Elizabeth tried to sound out Amanda about her feelings on any intimate subject, Amanda usually maneuvered around the topic and put her off completely.

Sometimes Elizabeth felt she had been used. She wondered if Amanda had written those nice letters simply as a way of getting Elizabeth to help her run away from New Brunswick. It was an awful feeling. Elizabeth thought it violated a trust that had been implied in their correspondence. Amanda in person seemed like a different girl than Amanda on paper.

"Señorita! Señorita Henley!"

She looked up at the front of the language lab. Her Spanish teacher was entreating her to put on the headphones. The lesson was beginning.

Elizabeth dragged through the class and the rest of the day. She saw Amanda in sixth-period honors English. Amanda smiled at her, but they barely said two words.

After school was out, they rode home together. Amanda asked her about helping with the homecoming dance decorations. Elizabeth told her that would be fine. She then tried to draw Amanda into a conversation about possible dates for the homecoming dance.

But Amanda didn't want to talk about boys, a topic that she had been obsessed with in her letters. Amanda wasn't concerned about a date. She was more interested in helping Elizabeth with the decorations.

Elizabeth should have been elated with Amanda's answer. Instead she was troubled by the fundamental coldness she sensed in her pen pal, and that perceptión would not go away.

As soon as they got home, Amanda went to her room and closed the door. Elizabeth studied in her own room for a while with Mr. Monkton at her side. When Mrs. Henley called them, they both came down to help her prepare dinner. Amanda was pleasant, though she did not talk very much to either one of them.

Mr. Henley arrived as they were setting the table. They all sat down to a nice meal. As they ate, Amanda seemed to come to life. She talked about the decorations committee for the homecoming dance. She was enthusiastic about the great job that Elizabeth was doing.

Elizabeth perked up a little. She talked about her ideas for different themes for the dance. Of course, the whole committee would have to vote, but Elizabeth wanted to have an old-time harvest-moon motif. They could decorate the gym like a barn and everyone could wear jeans and flannel shirts.

Amanda listened intently. She seemed to like the idea. But after dinner, when the table had been cleared and the dishes had been washed, she no longer wanted to talk about the dance. Amanda seemed distant, and, after doing her homework, claimed she was tired and wanted to go to bed early.

When Stephanie closed the door of her room, she let out a deep sigh. Except for Elizabeth's incessant efforts to become best friends, things were going fine in her charade. She wished Elizabeth would back off, leave her alone.

She couldn't warm up to Elizabeth. Try as she did, she couldn't be enthusiastic about her host's immature confessions and bubbly personality.

Elizabeth was the kind of girl that Stephanie had never gotten along with.

Stephanie could sense Elizabeth's growing frustration with her. But she figured it was best to keep her distance. If Elizabeth pressed Stephanie about her aloofness, she could always claim that schoolwork was keeping her busy.

On the whole, she had done well. She was actually learning something in her classes. Grades weren't due for another three weeks, but she was sure that she would pass all her classes. How could Miss Teen Perfect argue with that?

In her calculating mind, Stephanie was actually entertaining notions of going to college after she graduated. She had already met with her counselor to discuss applications. She was thinking about one of the big Midwestern universities, where she could lose herself. Also, she was beginning to consider getting a part-time job and moving away from the ideal family that the Henleys seemed to be.

"Just get through the school year and then it will all be over," she told herself.

As for Richard, he had backed off. Stephanie noticed him watching her from afar every so often, but they had said very little to each other since that first day. He had been pleasant but guarded, and Stephanie was worried that he was trying to find out about her. She wondered if she should try to get closer to him, just to find out what he knew.

Moving across the room, Stephanie stepped in front of the mirror. It was not her own face she saw there, but Amanda's. The sweet, naive face was pale and drawn. Tears ran down her cheeks. Stephanie gasped and put her hands over her eyes. She tried to cover her whole head and hide from the all-seeing mirror. When she dared to peek into the mirror once again, it was her own face she saw. And on her face she saw a look of desperation that she had never seen before. *Get ahold of yourself, Stephanie,* she told herself. *Get a grip on yourself.*

Undressing, Stephanie put on her pajamas and got into bed with her civics book. It was comforting to bury herself in her studies and block out the rest of the world. She liked reading herself to sleep.

But that night Stephanie had a dream that was not very comforting. In the dream, Stephanie found herself peering across the bank of a bubbling stream. Fog swirled through the trees.

A lilting voice came up through the fog. "Steph-a-nie!" The voice dragged out the syllables of her name, like a child calling to a friend.

"Steph-a-nie!"

Then the voice was quiet for a moment.

Stephanie looked down at the rocky bank of

the stream. Blood seeped between the brown stones. The crimson ooze turned into long red fingers that tried to grab at her ankles.

Stephanie leapt into the waters of the creek to get away from the fingers. Suddenly she was ankle-deep in blood. The stream flowed thick and red around her shins.

She jumped out of the creek onto the opposite bank. Her eyes peered at the ground. Nothing but rocks sat beneath her feet.

"Steph-a-nie!"

Fog swirled around her, ghostly vapor that billowed out of the trees. She wanted to run, but she found herself drawn toward the evergreens that were shrouded by the mist. Her feet followed a path. She stopped when she saw the low branches of the evergreens bending back to reveal freshly turned earth.

"I'm here, Steph-a-nie."

She started to take a step toward the grave. But suddenly the fresh earth began to shake, as if something beneath was trying to get out. Then the earth was swept away by a mysterious wind, and the frail, pathetic body of Amanda MacKenzie was revealed. Stephanie bent over to sweep the earth back over the body, but as fast as she could do it, the earth was blown away again.

Stephanie felt paralyzed, but she managed to turn and run. She dashed back toward the creek.

When she stepped on the opposite bank, the red fingers grabbed her feet, holding her in place.

"You can't run, Steph-a-nie." The voice was soft and soothing.

She looked back to see Amanda coming after her. The dead girl moved at a zombie's pace, staggering, with her arms outstretched.

Stephanie gasped and sat up in her bed. Sweat dripped from her face. The sheets were soaked with perspiration. Her hands were trembling. Her whole body shook with fear as she peered into the darkness.

"She's not going to get to me," Stephanie muttered.

Jumping out of bed, she switched on a light and peered into the mirror. For a second, she imagined that she saw the sad face of Amanda. But after a moment, she realized she was gazing at her own ashen countenance, staring back at herself with a dazed, frightened expression.

Chapter 13

"Are you all right?" Elizabeth asked, looking over at Amanda on the passenger side of the Escort. Her face was drawn, and she seemed lost in thought. They were on their way to school for an early meeting of the decorations committee.

"Amanda?"

"I'm okay," Amanda snapped.

"Oh. Sorry."

Amanda sighed. "I'm sorry. I didn't sleep well last night."

"Is anything the matter?" Elizabeth inquired.

"No. Nothing that A's and B's won't solve," Amanda said.

Elizabeth just nodded. She was still disappointed that she and her friend had not become closer. Her pen pal had been somebody who was sweet and eager and thoughtful. But the girl sitting next to her had wild mood swings and didn't share her thoughts and feelings. Sometimes she even thought that her pen pal and the girl staying at her house were two completely different people. After studying Amanda's letters, she had asked a few trick questions, but they had been answered correctly, even with some elaboration. But her guest never initiated discussions of her past. Elizabeth tried to be understanding, though. Amanda had had a hard life, and maybe the adjustment required to live with a new family and go to a new school was taking its toll. Just the same, she was worried.

Elizabeth guided the car into the parking lot. The lot was almost empty since it was so early. She and Amanda got out and walked to the cafeteria, where the meeting was being held. Trudy and three other people were already there.

The proceedings began immediately. Elizabeth, Trudy, and another girl, Carla, did most of the talking. Amanda sat quietly, staring out the window. Finally everyone began voting, yea or nay, on the theme Elizabeth suggested. But Amanda was still dreaming, oblivious of what was going on.

"Amanda?"

She did not respond immediately to her name.

"Amanda!"

Amanda glanced up. Elizabeth looked at her sternly.

"What?" Amanda asked blankly.

"We're taking a vote," Elizabeth told her.

"About my theme for the homecoming dance. You know, 'Shine On, Harvest Moon.' "

Amanda frowned. "Oh."

Trudy was staring at her. "What's wrong, Amanda?"

Amanda grimaced. "Well, Elizabeth's idea is okay. But it seems a little old-fashioned to me."

"That's the whole point," Elizabeth said testily.

"The nostalgia thing has been done to death," Amanda went on, avoiding Elizabeth's penetrating stare. "I mean, it's the nineties. We need something a little more trendy—you know, up-to-date."

Elizabeth was starting to look sick. "But I thought—"

"Maybe Amanda is right," Trudy chimed in. "What if we . . ."

The debate grew more heated. Amanda had opened a new can of worms. On the second vote, Elizabeth's idea was shot down in favor of a 'Top 40's Dance Party' theme. Everyone loved it except Elizabeth. She tried to be enthusiastic, but she couldn't believe that Amanda would be so mean to her.

For the rest of the day, Elizabeth fumed. She felt that Amanda had sabotaged her idea deliberately. When Elizabeth walked into sixth-period honors English, she didn't even look at Amanda.

They still had to ride home together after school. Amanda seemed cheerful as they drove through Cresswell. She didn't try to apologize for swaying the rest of the committee to vote against Elizabeth. She seemed heartless about the whole thing.

"So," she said, "looks like we're having a homecoming dance party."

Elizabeth glared over at her. "How could you do that to me, Amanda? I thought you liked my idea!"

She only shrugged. "Well, I did. At first. But somehow it didn't seem to fit with—"

"You sure picked a great time to trash it!"

"Hey," Amanda went on, "if the others had been sold on your idea, they wouldn't have changed their minds so easily. I mean, I just threw out a suggestion. And before I did, I said your idea was okay. It's not as if I spent hours trying to talk them out of the harvest-moon thing, Elizabeth!"

Elizabeth took a deep breath. She could see Amanda's point. The other members of the committee hadn't been overly excited about the nostalgia aspect of her idea. Maybe she had been trying to push it through too quickly.

"If it makes you feel any better," Amanda said at last, "I'm sorry. All right?"

Elizabeth sighed. "Okay," she said quietly.

When they got home, things were chilly. At dinner, Amanda explained the whole thing to Mr. and Mrs. Henley, acting more remorseful than she had been in the car. When her parents seemed to understand Amanda's point of view, Elizabeth tried to be gracious, though she was still upset.

After dinner, Amanda disappeared into her room and closed the door, leaving Elizabeth alone to ponder the strange, cold attitude of her ungrateful houseguest.

Stephanie was back in the fog. She could hear the bubbling creek in Arden Glen.

She approached the brook slowly and gazed down at its smooth surface. The water was clear and fresh. She walked along the path, toward the rich, dark earth beneath the evergreens. She brushed back the branches of the trees and peered down at the hole in the ground. It was empty.

Stephanie let go of the evergreen branches. She ran away from the grave. When she reached the brook, she stopped for a moment, listening for the sound of Amanda's eerie voice.

But the woods were silent. She glanced down at the clear waters of the stream. Suddenly the clear water turned blood red.

"Steph-a-nie," a hissing voice said accusingly.

Stephanie sucked in air and sat up in her bed. The nightmare had come again, for the second night in a row. She was quaking. Sweat had soaked through her nightclothes.

She wiped her forehead with the back of her hand. She sat in her bed for the rest of the night, unable to close her eyes. She was thinking of ways to make the horrible dream go away. By morning, she could come up with only one, unavoidable answer.

On Saturday morning, Elizabeth went off with her father to run some errands. Stephanie knew that ordinarily Elizabeth would have asked her to come along. But Elizabeth was in a snit, and it was just as well.

Stephanie was left alone with Mrs. Henley. After she helped with the breakfast dishes, Stephanie told Mrs. Henley that she was going out to shop for some of the decorations for the homecoming dance. Mrs. Henley didn't think twice about Stephanie going out on her own. After all, the girl had been in Cresswell for more than a month. She knew the town very well.

Stephanie called a pleasant farewell to Mrs. Henley and then bolted out the front door. She put on a pair of sunglasses and a beret to make sure she wasn't recognized as she made for the Cresswell bus station. Her plan was simple. She would return to the grave site, to make sure Amanda was still resting in the ground.

The round-trip fare to Porterville was only twelve dollars. Stephanie still had almost all the money she had started with—or that Amanda had started with.

When she arrived in Porterville, she went to the large map again to check her bearings. She considered taking a taxi to the woods, but that would mean a witness if anything happened to reveal the dead girl's whereabouts. She had to walk it. At least the day was bright and sunny. There was a cool crispness in the air. It was a beautiful fall day.

Stephanie walked quickly. She reached Arden Glen in ten minutes. When she saw the path, she hurried through the brush, toward the rushing sound of the stream.

Stephanie's skin crawled as she stood on the bank of the brook. It was just like the dreams she had been having, only the mists weren't there.

Slowly, she moved across the stream, heading up the trail toward the stand of evergreens. She had to see the grave. Her heart began to thump in her chest. Sweat broke out on her face, even though the air was cool in the shade.

She reached out toward the branches of the evergreens, half expecting a rotting hand to grab her wrist. When she brushed back the branches, something jumped at her. Stephanie screamed and leapt back. Then she saw a little brown rabbit hopping off into the forest. She breathed deeply, trying to regain her composure.

Pushing back the branches again, she peered down at the grave. The dark earth was still covered with a carpet of pine needles.

"I'm getting out of here."

She vaulted over the stream and raced down the path until she reached the highway. There, she stopped to pick off the briar thorns and bits of leaf that had stuck to her clothing. She didn't want to give herself away when she got back to Cresswell.

She reached the bus station in time to get the next bus out of town. She was back in the Cresswell bus station just after noon. Walking down the street, she felt confident that the dream would go away.

To cover herself in her story, she stopped and purchased a few rolls of crepe paper in pastel colors. When she came into the house, Mrs. Henley greeted her with a sweet smile. Later on, before dinner, she showed Elizabeth the crepe paper, and Elizabeth seemed to like it. But Elizabeth still seemed cool toward her, and Stephanie knew she would have to be extra nice to her over the next few days.

That night, Stephanie was a little worried about going to sleep. But she finally dropped off and slept like a baby. No nightmare haunted her. She awoke refreshed, happy that her plan had worked. She was free from her guilt. She had no idea that the real trouble would begin immediately after the homecoming dance.

Chapter 14

The Cresswell High School gymnasium was jumping. The steel rafters had been festooned with shiny streamers of multicolored crepe paper. A huge mirrored ball turned amid the streamers, reflecting the beams of two powerful spotlights.

On the stage at the rear of the gym, a professional disc jockey spun records and performed special mixes of lively songs from the fifties and sixties. The music was nonstop and the decor was flashy, giving the dance the atmosphere of a big-city club.

Beneath the whirling lights, the students celebrated a Top 40's Dance Party homecoming. The dancers were particularly boisterous since Cresswell had defeated Marshfield, 14–7, in the big homecoming game. Cresswell had been the underdog and hadn't been expected to win.

Along the east wall of the building stretched a long table that had been covered with refreshments. Behind the table, Elizabeth Henley worked feverishly to keep the punch bowls filled. Trudy and Amanda were also helping. It was a difficult job, since the majority of the student body had shown up for the dance.

"Hey, Liz," Trudy called. "Where is that other box of chocolate-chip cookies? I can't find it."

Elizabeth looked up from the punch bowl. "I think it's back in the storage closet, Trudy. Next to the coach's office."

Amanda pushed past Elizabeth. "I'll get it."

Elizabeth watched Amanda as she moved toward the rear of the gym. She was happy that Amanda had been so much nicer these past few days. Perhaps she was finally beginning to adjust. Elizabeth knew that it had been unreasonable for her to have expected them to be best friends right from the start. She reasoned that Amanda had come from the cold environment of her aunt and uncle's home. She could not be expected to warm up right away. But Elizabeth had decided not to give up on getting closer to Amanda. She was going to break through to the girl who had written her those nice letters.

Amanda came walking back toward her, carrying a big cardboard box of cookies. Elizabeth smiled warmly at her. Amanda smiled back and started to tug at the flaps of the box.

"Need some help?" Elizabeth asked.

Amanda shrugged. "Sure, why not?"

They opened the box and pulled out the

smaller boxes of cookies that were inside. Ripping open the packages, they dumped the cookies on paper plates and put the plates on the long table.

As soon as the refreshments were in place, Amanda announced, "I'll see if I can find some more."

Elizabeth touched her shoulder, stopping her. "Amanda?"

"Yes?"

Elizabeth felt herself blushing. "I just wanted to say that your idea was good. Everyone likes it, and the D.J. was a lot cheaper than a live band. He even brought his own sound system."

Amanda smiled weakly. "Sure. No problem."

"No," Elizabeth said. "I mean it. I'm sorry I got mad at you. You were right and I was just being stubborn. Okay?"

"Don't worry about it," said Amanda. "You don't have to apologize for anything." She turned and walked away. Elizabeth smiled, thinking that maybe this was the turning point in their relationship. Maybe now they could become close friends.

Laden with more cookies as well as a tray of canapés, Stephanie returned to the refreshment table. All evening she had been aware that Richard Tibbs was watching her. Now, as she arranged food and chatted with Elizabeth, Trudy, and a few other girls, she noticed Richard making his way toward her.

"It's going pretty well, isn't it?" exclaimed Trudy.

"Oh sure," Stephanie said absently, trying to figure out a way to hide from Richard.

"Go find somebody to dance with," said Trudy. "It's okay to leave us here."

"I might not have a choice," said Stephanie. "This is the moment I *haven't* been waiting for."

Trudy looked up. "What?"

"It's Richard Tibbs. I bet he's coming to ask me to dance. He never gives up."

"Oh, give him a break," Trudy said. "He's not so bad."

Richard walked up to the table. "Hi, Trudy, Amanda. You guys did great with the food. Hey, Trudy, want to dance?"

Stephanie sighed, thinking she was off the hook.

"No, I can't right now, Richard. Maybe Amanda wants to."

Stephanie frowned at her. "Trudy!"

Richard laughed pleasantly. "No, Amanda doesn't want to dance with me," he said.

Stephanie suddenly felt a tinge of guilt. She had been cold to all the boys at Cresswell High School. If she didn't show some interest in the opposite gender pretty soon, Elizabeth might become even more suspicious of her.

Richard started to turn and walk away. "Good night."

"Wait," Stephanie said. "I'd love to dance. C'mon." She came around from behind the table just as the D.J. put a slow tune on the turntable.

"Okay, Cresswell boys and girls, time to bring it down a notch with a number designed to get you a little closer together. . . ."

Richard grabbed Stephanie's hand and slipped his arm around her waist. "Don't worry. I won't get fresh."

They began to twirl around the gym floor. Stephanie was surprised to find that Richard was a good dancer. She closed her eyes and leaned closer to him, putting her face on his shoulder. Richard wrapped his other arm around her waist.

As Stephanie danced with him, she remembered some of the good times with Ted. It had been too long since she had embraced a member of the opposite sex. She had forgotten how good it felt to hold someone.

When the dance was over, she broke away from Richard. He looked down at Stephanie with moony eyes. She could see by the expression on his face that he was still hung up on her. It made her feel good, even though Richard had seemed menacing at one time. She still wasn't sure if he was intent upon discovering her deep, dark secret.

The D.J.'s voice boomed through the gym, breaking the romantic moment. "All right, Cresswell boys and girls, time to put a lid on this homecoming celebration. Time to bring the evening to an end. Just one more for the road. . . ."

A collective groan ran through the crowd. No one wanted to go home. The dance had been a big hit.

Stephanie gave Richard a little kiss on the cheek. He blushed. He actually turned red right there in front of her. "I have to go, Richard," she said.

"But—"

"We have to clean up," she told him, turning on her heel.

"Wow," Trudy said when Stephanie got back to the refreshment table. "What did you do to Richard? He looks like he's sick."

Stephanie shrugged. "I just danced with him."

"Okay," Elizabeth said. "Let's break this puppy down. The sooner we clean up, the sooner we get out of here. Hey, Richard! Want to help?"

Stephanie grimaced. "Elizabeth!"

But Richard was already coming toward them. "Sure, I'd be happy to give you a hand."

* * *

An hour later the last dance was but a memory, and the final few stragglers were passing through the large double doors of the gymnasium into the cool night air.

"Well," Richard said. "We did it."

Everything was broken down and put away. The trash had been bagged, the tables were folded up. All of the leftovers had been stored.

Trudy pointed up at the ceiling. "What about the tinsel and the streamers?"

Elizabeth shrugged. "Maintenance will take care of that. They have the high ladders."

Stephanie sighed. "It was nice, even if I do say so myself."

"Yeah," Richard said, slipping next to Stephanie like a frisky puppy dog. "Your idea was the best, Amanda."

Stephanie was beginning to feel sorry that she had encouraged him. It was obvious that he wanted to be closer to her. But even in the guise of Amanda, she would never go for an immature boy like Richard Tibbs.

Elizabeth stretched, working out some of the stiffness in her shoulders. "I should be tired, but I'm charged. Anybody feel like going for burgers? I'm starving. I didn't eat any of that food we were shoveling tonight."

Trudy nodded. "I'm not tired either. What time is it?"

Richard looked at his watch. "Twelve-thirty. I think the Tri-City Diner is still open."

"Great," Elizabeth replied. "I can call Mom and tell her we're going to be late. There's a pay phone at the diner."

Stephanie frowned. "I don't know, Elizabeth." She didn't want to get stuck with Richard.

"Oh, come on," Elizabeth said. "It'll be fun."

"I'm buying," Richard chimed in. "You can ride with me, Amanda."

Stephanie sighed, seeing that there was no way out. "Oh, all right."

They left the gymnasium. Trudy got into the Escort with Elizabeth. Stephanie had to ride in Richard's Camaro. He talked all the way to the diner. Stephanie listened politely until they were sitting in the booth at the diner. She was glad when Elizabeth and Trudy joined them, saving her from being alone with Richard. They picked up their menus and began to talk about the evening.

It was then that Stephanie looked over the top of her menu and saw something that made her go pale.

"What is it?" Elizabeth asked.

"Nothing," Stephanie replied, hiding behind the menu again. "I think I drank too much of that punch at the dance."

She couldn't tell them the real reason for her

consternation. Trouble had just walked through the front door of the diner. And his name was Ted Dorak, Stephanie's old boyfriend and former partner in crime.

Chapter 15

As Ted glanced around the diner, Stephanie ducked behind the menu, pretending to study the diner's fare. Ted eased onto a stool at the counter and picked up a menu. Stephanie looked at him again to make sure that he wasn't looking in her direction.

"I think I'll have the pizza burger," Trudy said.

Elizabeth wrinkled her nose. "Suddenly I kind of feel like having breakfast. Eggs or pancakes maybe."

Richard closed his menu. "I'm going for the chili burger. What are you going to have, Amanda?"

Stephanie put the menu on the table. "I'm not sure." She glanced toward the counter again to see Ted sipping a cup of coffee. She had to move fast.

"Better decide," Richard said. "Here comes the waitress."

Stephanie started to slide out of the booth.

"You guys go ahead and order. I have to go to the rest room."

She walked toward the back of the diner. Her plan was simple. She would climb out of the bathroom window and walk back to the Henley house. When the others asked her about it later, she would say that she had gotten sick to her stomach and then departed for home through the back door so she wouldn't spoil everyone's good time. She didn't care how bizarre it seemed to them. She had to get away before Ted saw her.

The bathroom window was open. Stephanie climbed out, emerging in back of the diner. She started slowly toward the parking lot. If she was lucky, she might find a taxi and save herself the long walk home.

Turning the corner, Stephanie stopped for a moment to survey the parking lot. Elizabeth's car was thirty feet away from her. Maybe it would be better if she just climbed in the back seat and stayed low for a while. Sooner or later Elizabeth would come out. Stephanie could give her the story about being sick.

Stephanie took a step away from the corner of the building. Suddenly a cold hand closed around her wrist. She turned to see Ted lurching out of the shadows. He grabbed her other wrist and pulled her close to him.

"Let go of me," Stephanie snapped. "I'll scream."

Ted grinned at her. Sharp creases cut across his rough face. "What, no hello?"

"I mean it, Ted. I'll scream bloody murder."

"No you won't, Steph. You don't want your little friends to see you with me. That's why you snuck out the bathroom window. I was the one who taught you that trick. Remember? We ducked a lot of restaurant tabs together."

"Leave me alone, Ted. I mean it."

His face came closer. "I missed you, Steph. Why'd you leave me?"

She stopped struggling and glared at him. "Can't you guess?"

"No, I want to hear you say it."

"Because I got tired of your dead-end life," Stephanie replied. "I was sick of your attitude."

A hurt expression spread over Ted's face. "Hey, I'd never do anything to hurt you. And you ran out on me, not the other way around."

She tried a more pleading tone. "Ted, you've got to leave me alone. Things have changed. I've got it good now. Don't blow it for me."

Ted laughed. "Ha! I knew you had some kind of scam going. Why else would you be hanging with those high-school geeks?"

"Ted—"

"Let me in on it, Steph. Share the wealth. Give me a piece of the action."

"This isn't like that, Ted," she said, still trying to break free.

"Gimme a kiss!"

"No—"

He pressed his mouth to hers, trying to kiss her. Stephanie fought him. She wasn't going to get taken in again. Ted was a loser.

Finally she broke away. She glared into his swarthy face. "Leave me alone, Ted."

He pointed a finger at her. "What if I blow the little scam you've got going here?"

"It's not a scam," Stephanie replied. "I'm finally making good. I'm back in school and I—"

"Amanda?"

She looked around to see Elizabeth standing behind them.

A devious smile crept over Ted's thin mouth. "Amanda, huh?"

Elizabeth moved closer, squinting at the hulking figure of the man in the leather motorcycle jacket. "Amanda, are you all right?"

Stephanie smiled at Elizabeth and then looked into Ted's hostile eyes. "Yes, I'm fine. I felt a little sick, but I'm okay now. This gentleman was just helping me. Isn't that right, sir?"

"Yeah," Ted replied. "I was just helping her."

Elizabeth frowned at her. "Do you want to go home?"

Stephanie moved away from Ted. "Yes, I would."

Elizabeth studied Ted and then looked at Stephanie. "Do you know him?"

Stephanie shook her head. "No. He was just nice enough to help me. We have to be going now." She turned to Ted. "Thank you," she said with a look in her eyes that pleaded with him not to reveal her identity.

"Sure, *Amanda,*" Ted replied. "See you around."

Stephanie turned away, taking Elizabeth's arm. "Sorry, Elizabeth. Let's go home."

Elizabeth put her arm around her. "Are you sure you're all right?"

"Yes, I just needed some air."

Once they had reached the cars, Elizabeth spoke. "Amanda, I have to take Trudy home. Do you mind riding with Richard?"

"No, not at all."

Anything to get away from the hulking shadow of Ted Dorak.

"I don't know, Trudy," Elizabeth said as she drove her friend home. "She acted like she knew him. I mean, they were arguing or something."

Trudy grimaced. "Get real. Amanda and some kind of motorcycle thug? She'd never go for someone like that."

Elizabeth sighed. "I can't understand it. When we were writing back and forth, she seemed like the sweetest girl in the world. But she's acted—I don't know, different, since she got here. I thought it was some kind of adjustment problem and that finally she was getting over it. But now I don't know."

"You can't tell about someone from their letters, Liz," Trudy offered.

Elizabeth turned her car onto Marston Street, heading for Trudy's house in the Upper Basin, a neighborhood of mostly two-family houses. She had to talk to someone.

"I thought we were going to be close," Elizabeth went on. "But she shuts me out every time we try to talk."

Trudy frowned at her. "You know what I think?"

"What?"

"I think you're jealous, Liz. Amanda's staying with you, but she's determined to have her own life and you can't stand it."

Elizabeth sighed. "Maybe you're right, Trudes. Maybe you're right."

She dropped Trudy off and started to drive home. As she drove down Congress Street, a motorcycle whizzed around her, crossing a double line. It looked like the same guy Amanda had been talking to in the parking lot of the diner.

Elizabeth shook her head, trying to interpret

the anxious feeling she had about the girl who was living with her.

All the way home, Stephanie listened to Richard talk. He was a bundle of energy and Stephanie knew why. Richard wanted another kiss at the door before they said good night. His hopes had been bolstered by the dance they had shared.

But Stephanie was still on edge from her run-in with Ted. Blind luck had led her old boyfriend to the Tri-City Diner just when Stephanie and the others were there. She wondered what Ted had been doing lately, and if he would be able to find out where she was living. He had heard Elizabeth call her Amanda, and that must have set evil little wheels turning in his head.

"Anyway, the coach had me relieve Wilkens in the third inning," Richard went on. "There were two men on. This was my first chance . . ."

Stephanie wasn't listening. She couldn't get Ted out of her mind.

Finally Richard braked the car in front of the Henleys' house. "Well, here we are." He got out, going to her side to open the door.

Stephanie sighed. She didn't want to play the little scene at the door. But Richard was determined. He even put his hand on her shoulder as they walked up the front steps.

Stephanie took the hand off her shoulder and looked up at him. "Richard, I—"

But he was already lowering his face, trying to kiss her.

"Richard—"

"Hey, you kissed me at the dance. I thought we could be friends, Amanda?"

Stephanie was about to give him a rough time when she heard the motorcycle roaring down the street. It slowed in front of the house. As Ted gunned the engine, Stephanie grabbed Richard and pressed her lips to his. The motorcycle moved on, disappearing around the corner.

Stephanie broke away.

Richard gawked at her. "Amanda, I—" He tried to come back for more.

Stephanie pushed him away and smiled. "That's enough for one night."

"Sure, I—I mean, gosh."

She watched him strutting back to his car. He turned one last time to wave and smile. Stephanie waved back just to get rid of him.

When he was gone, she shook her head and sighed. She figured that Ted and Richard were both going to be trouble.

Chapter 16

"Welcome to the gates of hell, Stephanie. We've been waiting for you."

Stephanie sat up in bed. Her covers had been thrown off. She was soaked through with sweat. The dream had returned. She knew it had something to do with Ted's arrival the night before.

"Amanda!"

She really heard the voice. It wasn't a dream this time. A light tap sounded on her door. It was Elizabeth who was calling to her.

"Amanda, it's me. Are you awake?"

Stephanie drew a deep breath. "What?"

"Amanda, you have a telephone call."

Stephanie's stomach turned. "Who is it?"

"A guy," Elizabeth replied. "I didn't get his name."

"Ted," Stephanie whispered to herself.

Who else would be calling her on Saturday morning? She climbed out of bed and put on a robe.

"Amanda—"

She opened the door and pushed past Elizabeth. "It's under control."

Elizabeth watched Amanda disappear down the stairs. She started to turn away, but then she hesitated when she saw the open door. Elizabeth's heart began to pound. She realized that she had not been in the third-floor bedroom since the day of Amanda's arrival. Elizabeth saw her chance. Ordinarily, she was not the kind to sneak around. But this was an opportunity to allay or to substantiate some of her suspicions. She pushed through the door and stepped into the room.

Stephanie picked up the phone. "Hello?" she said gruffly.

"Hi, Amanda."

She didn't immediately recognize the voice. "Who is this?"

"Me. Richard."

Stephanie rolled her eyes. "What do *you* want?"

Richard hesitated at the other end of the line. "Hey, what's wrong?"

"I had a bad dream. And it's early, isn't it?"

"It's eight-thirty," came the eager voice. "I wanted to catch you before you went out."

"Well, you did."

"Hey, I thought we might do something this

afternoon," Richard said excitedly. "We could go to a movie."

"I'm busy," Stephanie replied.

"Amanda, we had a nice evening. I thought everything was really good with us." He had adopted a pleading tone.

"Richard," she hissed into the phone, "I'm sure we'll go out sometime, but I just don't want to be pestered. Good-bye."

She put down the phone firmly. As she turned toward the stairs, she saw Mr. Henley staring at her with narrow eyes. Stephanie tried to smile, but she was sure he had heard the whole thing.

"Good morning, Mr. Henley."

"Everything all right, Amanda?"

"Yes," she replied. "It's just that this boy won't leave me alone."

He nodded understandingly. "Well, I'm sure he won't bother you after that tongue-lashing you just gave him."

"No, sir. I suppose I shouldn't have been so rude to him." She tried to laugh and act as Amanda would in such a situation.

Mr. Henley shrugged. "Well, sometimes that's what it takes. Say, we're all going over to New Castle to my sister's house. We're going to stay the night, so we won't be back until tomorrow evening. Would you like to come along?"

"I'd rather not, if that's all right with you," she

replied. "Thanks anyway. I have a lot of school work."

"Well, you'll have the house to yourself while we're gone."

"Yes, sir. I'll make sure everything is okay."

And I have to go back to Arden Glen, she thought. *I have to visit the grave again and make the nightmare go away.*

Elizabeth wasn't sure what she was looking for in Amanda's room. But her doubts had to be dealt with. When she spotted Amanda's history notebook sitting on the desk, she raced over to it.

Of course! she thought. Why hadn't she thought of it before? She could look at Amanda's handwriting and compare it to the letters that she had written. She was reaching for the notebook when she heard steps behind her.

"What are you doing in here?"

Elizabeth turned to see Amanda's glaring face. "I was just going to look at your history notes. I'm sorry."

Amanda's face softened slightly. "Oh. Well, you can look at them later. Your father wants to see you downstairs."

Elizabeth nodded. "Sure. Are you coming to New Castle?"

"No," Amanda replied blandly. "I've got too much studying to do."

Elizabeth left the room, heading downstairs. Her doubts had grown even bigger when she saw Amanda's scowling expression. But she would have to wait a little longer before her suspicions were put to the test.

Richard Tibbs parked his mother's Camaro down the street from the Henleys' house and waited. Amanda had been so affectionate to him the night before, after all those weeks of being cold and distant. But on the phone this morning she had been stand-offish and rude, just like she had been on their first day at school. After feeling her sweet lips on his the evening before, he knew that she liked him. He wasn't going to be pushed aside now. Something was troubling her. She needed his help. She was crying out to him in desperation from the bottom of her sweet, vulnerable soul. He was going to be there for her.

After sitting for an hour, Richard saw the Henleys' car pull out of the driveway. He looked closely and saw Mr. and Mrs. Henley in the front seat and Elizabeth in the back seat. Where was Amanda? Had she been as rude to her hosts as she had been to him? Something was strange about Amanda. What could her secret be? From that first day he had known something was wrong, but he could never figure it out. Today he would find out. He would help her with whatever problems were tormenting her, and she would reward him with the sweetest affection he had ever known.

Finally, his patience was rewarded. Amanda emerged from the house and hurried down the front walk. Richard carefully tailed her for twenty minutes. She was walking quickly and seemed sure of where she was going. Richard was grateful. It made her easier to follow. She led him all the way to the bus station. At the entrance, she looked around as if she feared she was being followed. And then she disappeared inside.

Stephanie glanced out of the bus window, thinking about all the loose ends that had cropped up to haunt her. Ted had met her by accident, bringing back the dreams. Richard had gotten the wrong idea about her and wanted to be her boyfriend. And Elizabeth was now snooping about in her room.

"Elizabeth," she muttered to herself. Elizabeth was going to be the real problem. She had been growing more suspicious every day. Stephanie would have to do something, maybe try to be a better friend to her. Maybe confide in her? No, that wouldn't work. She could always leave. But that would be hard to do after putting so much effort into school and getting a new start in life.

"Porterville!"

When Stephanie got off the bus, she headed straight for Arden Glen. She reached the woods in ten minutes.

The fall foliage was peaking in the forest. Red, orange, and yellow hues sparkled in the tree-tops. Stephanie was worried that she would not be able to find the path again. But suddenly there it was, leading back toward the bubbling creek that had plagued her dreams.

Stephanie started back into the forest, walking under the sun-shimmered colors of the fall leaves. She saw the brook ahead of her. She crossed it, heading for the grave, stopping when she saw the evergreens. She stood there for a long time, wondering what to do. She knew she had to look at the grave again. Maybe she should take the whole thing a step further and actually look at the dead body.

"I can't bear to have another dream," she said to herself.

She moved toward the grave, throwing back the unchanged green branches. The straw-colored needles still covered the soft earth. She swept away the needles with her hand.

"Just do it and get it over with."

Stephanie was starting to dig when she heard

a twig snap behind her. She looked back, gaping at the shadow that moved in her direction.

"I don't know," Elizabeth said to her mother and father. "There's something strange about Amanda. She doesn't really seem like the girl who wrote all those letters."

Mrs. Henley frowned. "Really? Hmm. Maybe you're right. I once asked her about some of the towns in New Brunswick and she seemed vague and evasive, as if she really didn't know anything about them. The only reason I know is because we spent a few summers up near Campobello before you were born."

Mr. Henley nodded thoughtfully. "You know, she was really giving it to some boy on the phone today. Don't ask me what it was all about, but I saw another side of her that I'm not sure I liked."

Elizabeth leaned forward, looking over into the front seat. "I was thinking. Maybe we should call her aunt and uncle."

Mrs. Henley nodded. "Not a bad idea."

"We can do that," Mr. Henley replied. "But it'll have to wait until Monday morning. That okay with you, Liz? I don't want your Aunt Connie getting worked up."

Elizabeth leaned back, watching as the car drew closer to her aunt's house in New Castle. "Yes, that'll be all right."

Of course, a call to New Brunswick would uncover their scheme. But Elizabeth didn't care. Suddenly she no longer wanted Amanda Mac-Kenzie living under the same roof with the Henley family.

Chapter 17

From the coffee shop across the street from the Cresswell bus station, Richard had seen Amanda get on the bus to Porterville. He drove to the Porterville bus station and waited. When Amanda disembarked at the station he tailed her out to Arden Glen. He had followed her into the woods.

"Is this what you had to do this afternoon?" he asked when she turned and saw him.

Amanda stood up quickly, wiping the dirt from her hands. "Richard! What are you doing here?"

"I want to help you," Richard said. "Everything was so nice with us last night."

Amanda glared at him. "Get real."

Richard wasn't listening. He had to talk. It helped calm his nerves. "You waited until the Henleys took off before you left the house. Why's that, Amanda?"

Amanda moved out into the clearing. "What do you want, Richard?"

Richard peered back under the branches of the evergreens. "Are you a nature lover, Amanda?"

"That's none of your business," Amanda snapped.

Richard frowned. "Oh, I think it *is* my business. See, I watched you go into the bus station. I looked really carefully to see which bus you took. Then I drove ahead and waited for you to get off at Porterville. I don't understand why you came all the way out here."

Amanda tried to push around him. "I'm leaving."

Richard grabbed her. "Wait a minute. I can help you. You were about to dig there. What were you looking for?"

She shrugged. "Nothing. I just like this place. A friend brought me here."

"Who?" he asked quickly.

"Just—just a friend."

He tried to look over her shoulder again. "A friend who's back there under those branches?" He didn't know why he said that, but suddenly he knew what the answer was. He started to move toward the evergreen branches.

Amanda stopped him. "No. There's nothing back there. I was just looking for mushrooms. My friend told me that I could find mushrooms back here."

"Mushrooms? I don't believe it. I want to look for myself."

She stared at him hard, up close. "What do you really want, Richard?"

"You're in trouble, and I want to help you. I've told you." Richard could feel her terror and confusion, but he was not to be dissuaded.

They stared at each other for a moment, then she said, "Okay, let's dig. I'll show you my little secret."

Together they started brushing away the pine needles and dirt. Richard was breathing quickly, horrified by the thought of what he might see, but exhilarated by his intimacy with Amanda. She was going to let him in on her secret. Now, at last, he could save her.

When they got down to the rocks, Richard paused and looked at his companion. "What's that smell, Amanda? It's disgusting. Do you have something buried here?"

She looked at him and smiled. "My name's not Amanda, Richard. It's Stephanie. Amanda is down here. Look." Hurriedly, she threw a few of the rocks aside and directed Richard's wide eyes to a certain part of the grave.

Richard looked intently, and when he saw the inert body beneath the dirt and pine needles his stomach began to rumble. When the rock was smashed against his head, he fell forward into the shallow void of Amanda's grave.

*   *   *

Stephanie had to think quickly. She piled the
stones, dirt, and pine needles over Richard and
raced out into the clearing. Then she heard
voices echoing through the woods. Were they
real voices, or was she going crazy? She listened.
There was more than one and they seemed to be
coming straight for her.

Stephanie panicked. She did not even consider hiding in the trees. The risk of discovery
was too great. The voices grew louder behind
her. Stephanie jumped the creek and flew up
the path, making for the road.

When she emerged from Arden Glen, she saw
Richard's Camaro sitting by the highway. She
thought about taking the car, but she realized
she did not have the keys. She began to walk
toward town, praying that no one would see her.

Every time she heard a car coming down the
road, Stephanie leapt back into the woods, hiding. She finally got to Porterville without being
seen. As soon as she ran into the bus station, she
checked the schedule, seeing that she had
missed the bus. There wasn't another departure
for two hours.

"What am I going to do?"

She took a deep breath. She could leave, head
away from the area, try to find a new start. But
she would need money and her clothes.

The Henleys weren't coming back until Sunday night. She could go back to Cresswell and take what she needed. She knew that Mr. Henley kept some money in the top drawer of his dresser. If she left town Saturday night, she would have a full day to run before it was discovered that she was missing.

Her nerves were jangling. She sat down in one of the television chairs, the kind that required twenty-five cents for fifteen minutes of viewing. Stephanie fought the trembling that spread through her body. Then she saw the policeman walking toward her.

"Excuse me, miss."

She looked up at him. "Yes?" she replied in a squeaky voice.

"You're not supposed to sit there unless you're going to watch television," the officer replied. "It's the rules of the station."

Stephanie reached into her pockets, taking out two quarters. "Sorry," she said. "I didn't know."

She dropped the quarters in the slot. The black-and-white television glowed to life. Stephanie began to look at the screen. The policeman wandered off without noticing her disheveled appearance.

"Got to clean up."

She hurried to the same bathroom where she had changed her identity before. After she had washed her hands and face, she went to the refreshment stand and bought a soft drink. She also asked for more quarters to put in the television.

Sitting in the chair again, she sipped the soda and focused her eyes on the gray screen. She did not really listen to the program that was playing. She only wanted to look like anyone else waiting for a bus. Her eyes kept flickering to the clock on the wall. Time was moving too slowly for Stephanie.

"Come on!"

She still had an hour to wait. She dropped more quarters into the television. She squirmed for another thirty minutes before the news report broke into the program on the screen.

"Good afternoon, I'm Scott Roman with a special bulletin just in from Porterville. The bodies of a young Cresswell man and a young woman were discovered today in Arden Glen."

Stephanie gaped at the screen. *Already?* she thought. The hikers must have discovered the grave shortly after she had run.

". . . named Richard Tibbs, a senior at Cresswell High. The body of the young woman has been identified as Stephanie Rendall . . ."

"Me?"

Of course! She had buried her own identification with Amanda. They believed that Stephanie was the girl in the grave.

". . . connection between Tibbs, who died

recently, and the badly decomposed body is thought by authorities to be a bizarre twist on a murder-suicide . . ."

Stephanie let out a short laugh. She couldn't believe it. She was off the hook, at least for now.

". . . police are saying that Tibbs must have killed the girl four or five weeks ago and then returned to the site and killed himself because of his own guilt."

But what else would they think? She hadn't left anything behind to incriminate Amanda MacKenzie. She could go back to Cresswell and pick up where she had left off. Who would suspect her? She could deny any knowledge of Richard's activities. After all, she had just turned down his invitation for a date. Elizabeth would testify that Amanda had always thought Richard was a creep.

". . . none of Stephanie Rendall's family has been located . . ."

"Attention passengers. Now leaving for Cresswell and points south . . ."

Stephanie was beaming when she climbed onto the bus. She knew she would have to show grief after she "learned" of Richard's suicide. Elizabeth would be the toughest to convince. Stephanie might have to work on her for a while.

She rode the bus back to Cresswell and walked home. She didn't know how bad her troubles were until she stepped into the

Henleys' house. She could hear the television blaring in the living room.

"Elizabeth?"

There was no answer.

Stephanie moved through the hall, emerging in the living room. Someone sat in Mr. Henley's easy chair. But when she saw the motorcycle boots, she knew it wasn't Elizabeth's father.

"You!"

Ted grinned at her. "Stephanie!"

She glared at him. "How did you get in here?"

"Hey, Steph, you know me. Ted Dorak is the best at breaking and entering."

She pointed toward the door. "Get out. Get out now!"

He laughed. "Aw, come on, Stephanie. Oh, wait. You're Amanda. Stephanie's dead. They found her in a place called—what was it? Arden Glen?"

Her eyes grew wide. "You don't have anything on me!"

He stood up. "No? I think you're wrong, Steph —I mean, Amanda. See, I was just about to blow this town. I would have been out of here tomorrow. Only the place I'm staying has a cheap television in the room. So I see this report, oh, I'd say about an hour ago. I figure, Steph offed this Amanda and took her place. It made sense to me. That's why you weren't very glad to see your old Ted."

"You're a creep, Ted."

He threw out his hands. "Hey, I'm not a murderer. Compared to you, I'm a saint. But I've got to hand it to you, Steph. You've got guts."

She sighed, realizing that there was no way for her to win. "What do you want from me, Ted?"

"Cash." He looked around the room. "This place smells of it."

"I'll need time," she replied. "I can take the old man for a bundle, but you have to give me a few days."

He eyed her suspiciously. "I don't know if I can trust you now. I mean, you're a killer."

She moved toward him, sliding her hands along his chest. She had to humor him. "If you want me to score big, I need time," she cooed.

He smiled a little.

She kissed him for a long time and then broke away. "I'm tired of this place anyway, Ted. Where do you want to go?"

"West," he said. "Or south. Doesn't matter. Listen, are you sure you can do this deal?"

"I'm sure," she replied.

"Okay," Ted said. "You've got till Monday. But if you don't come through, I'll blow the whistle and you'll fry, Steph. You'll fry big time."

Chapter 18

On Monday morning, Elizabeth sat down with her parents at the breakfast table. She was sad about Richard Tibbs. Elizabeth had never been overly fond of Richard, but she had liked him enough to be sorry that he was dead. She still couldn't believe he had killed that girl, let alone himself.

Mr. Henley frowned at his daughter. "Elizabeth, honey, are you all right?"

She nodded. "I'm just thinking about Richard."

Mr. Henley sighed. "Bad business. Killed her and then himself."

Mrs. Henley glanced toward the stairs. "Where's Amanda?"

"In her room," Elizabeth replied. "She's not going to school today."

"Wasn't she seeing that boy?" Mr. Henley asked.

"Sort of," Elizabeth replied. "But she always felt uncomfortable around him. I guess she was right."

Mrs. Henley patted her daughter's hand. "Why don't you go check on her?"

"Okay, Mom. But I was thinking. Maybe we should put off calling her aunt and uncle. They never did have a good relationship with her. It might upset her more if she heard from them." She wanted to make the call without her parents knowing. If her suspicions proved to be correct, she wanted to work out the solution on her own.

"I think you're right, honey," Mrs. Henley replied. "It can wait."

Elizabeth rose from the table and walked upstairs. Just below the second-floor landing, she stopped when she heard Amanda's voice. Amanda was having a frantic conversation with someone on the telephone extension. Elizabeth listened.

"No, no. Listen to me. I'll have the money. I'm taking the northbound bus at noon. . . . What? . . . Don't worry about her. If Elizabeth gets in my way, she'll get what the other two got. . . ."

Elizabeth crept back down the stairs. She kissed her mother good-bye and went out to her car. She drove to school, and when she arrived, she headed straight for the school auditorium, where members of the drama club were rehearsing a scene from the winter production before classes began. She knew what she had to do.

She was going to find her old friend Carol Leeds. Elizabeth hadn't socialized with Carol very much since their freshman year, but their friendship was intact. Elizabeth was sure that her mysterious houseguest had never met Carol, and she was well aware of Carol's acting abilities, which made her a crucial factor in Elizabeth's plans.

"I'm going out, Amanda!" Mrs. Henley called. "Do you want anything?"

Stephanie cracked open the door. "No, ma'am. Thank you anyway."

"There's fruit and muffins in the fridge, Amanda. You should try to eat something for breakfast."

"Yes, ma'am. I will."

Stephanie stood by the door, fully dressed. She was ready to move, but there was still a lot to do before she left Cresswell.

When she heard the door slam downstairs, she moved out of the room, carrying one suitcase and a canvas tote bag. Now she had to finish her plan.

On the second floor, she stepped into the Henleys' bedroom. She opened a drawer and reached in to grab a zippered leather pouch from under Mr. Henley's underwear. She had seen him take cash from it one evening. She unzipped the pouch and counted a green roll of ten fifty-dollar bills and another roll of ten tens.

There was six hundred dollars in all, enough to take her away from Cresswell to find a new start.

She put the money back into the pouch, dropped it into the canvas tote bag, and trotted down the stairs and out of the house. At the corner, she called a cab and waited for it in a nearby coffee shop. Today was no day to be seen out on the streets, walking to the bus station.

Chapter 19

As the bus rolled out of Cresswell, Stephanie looked out the window. She was ready to break out. When she got to Cape Cod, she would hang out for a day and then take off again. No one would expect her to head there.

"Excuse me. Excuse me, miss."

Stephanie turned to see a young woman smiling at her. "Yes?"

"Do you have change for a fifty?" the girl asked.

Stephanie's eyes grew wide when she saw that the girl's wallet was full of money. "Yes, I do. Here."

She counted out five tens from the money in the pouch.

"Thank you," the girl said. "I want to get something at the next stop and the snack bar people don't like to take a fifty."

Stephanie nodded, sizing up the innocent-looking young woman. "So, are you heading to Cape Cod?"

"Why, yes," the girl replied, "I am. Are you?"

Stephanie nodded. "I hear it's nice this time of year."

"Yes, I hear the same thing."

"Are you going to visit family?" Stephanie asked.

"No, I'm just getting away for a few days."

Stephanie smiled. "Me, too. My name is Amanda."

"Carol. Nice to meet you."

Stephanie shifted to the aisle seat, moving closer to Carol. "It's a long ride, Carol. I'm not much of a talker, but I do like to listen."

"You'd better watch it," Carol replied humorously. "I'll talk your ear off."

"I'm counting on it," Stephanie said. "Tell me your whole life story. And don't leave out a single detail."

Stephanie thought she had found a gold mine. She was not going to assume the girl's identity, the way she had with Amanda MacKenzie. That ruse had been her biggest mistake.

Instead, she was going to kill her and take her money. She was going to do the same thing all over the country. It made sense. She could travel, change her looks at every stop so she would not be identified. She was going to hunt like the lioness, taking her prey where she found it.

"Have you ever seen the Cape?" Carol asked.

"No," Stephanie replied. "But I'm going to stay a while. Maybe we could sightsee together."

"Sure," Carol replied. "Walk along the beach, explore the dunes. It'll be great."

Stephanie saw herself clubbing the girl at the earliest opportunity. She would take her money and leave on the next bus out. By the time they found the body, she would be long gone.

"Porterville," the driver called.

"I have an idea," said Stephanie. "Let's get off here and have a picnic. We can catch the next bus in an hour. What do you say?"

"Sure," said Carol eagerly. "Aren't you nice to suggest that. Where should we go?"

"Don't worry," offered Stephanie. "There's a big park around here. There are lots of picnic spots."

As they stepped off the bus, Carol turned to Stephanie. "I'll be back in a jiffy. I have to use the rest room."

"Sure," replied Stephanie. "I'll meet you over near the vending machines." Spotting Ted waiting eagerly at the end of the receiving platform, she made a quick signal for him to hang back. Ted was planning to accompany her to Cape Cod. But Stephanie had other plans.

When Carol had trotted off, she motioned for Ted to come over. He walked slowly, a big smirk on his face.

"Got the money, Steph?" he asked.

"Hold your horses," she told him excitedly. "That girl's carrying Fort Knox with her. I'm taking her on a picnic. Make yourself scarce. I'll meet you back here in an hour."

He looked at her thoughtfully for a moment. She knew he didn't trust her, but he was too stupid to think of an alternative plan. Anyhow, she was confident she could deal with Ted easily enough when the time came.

"Okay," he said. "I'll be an innocent by-stander and watch some TV." He ambled over to one of the television chairs, pushed a few quarters into the slot, and tuned in a game show.

"Here's the tape," said Carol, handing over the small cassette player to the other girl in the restroom. "She wants to take me on a picnic. How did I do?"

"You did great," exclaimed Elizabeth. "Now go on out there and tell her you want to sit down for a minute. It's almost over."

Carol did as she was instructed. Elizabeth followed ten seconds later. She positioned herself at the entrance to the passageway leading to the restrooms and nodded to the three men in business suits.

"Come on," said Stephanie to her suddenly tired victim. "Let's get going." She stood up and a detective's badge was thrust into her face by a beefy, manicured hand. She gasped and sat down again. She looked up as her Miranda rights were being read and saw Elizabeth staring at her. Then Elizabeth turned and walked away, with Carol at her side.

Thirty feet away, Ted was dragged out of the television chair by two pairs of strong hands. His eyes were affixed to the smiling game-show contestant who had just won $25,000 by correctly naming the location of the Irrawaddy River.